Bhaskar Som, a management consultant by profession, has over thirty years of cross-sector experience in corporate advisory, strategy formulation, risk management, data analytics and climate change. He is a Global Association of Risk Professionals (GARP)-certified financial risk manager and a sustainability and climate risk champion.

Over the years, Bhaskar has been fortunate to extensively travel across India and the world. These travels have helped him understand and appreciate different cultures and connect with people from diverse backgrounds, making him realise that human development is a story of migration and a family's identity is always evolving. This novel is an attempt to drive home this point.

Bhaskar holds a postgraduate degree in management from IIM Calcutta and a bachelor's degree in mechanical engineering from IIT Madras. He currently resides in Mumbai.

Bengal Region of the Sixteenth century

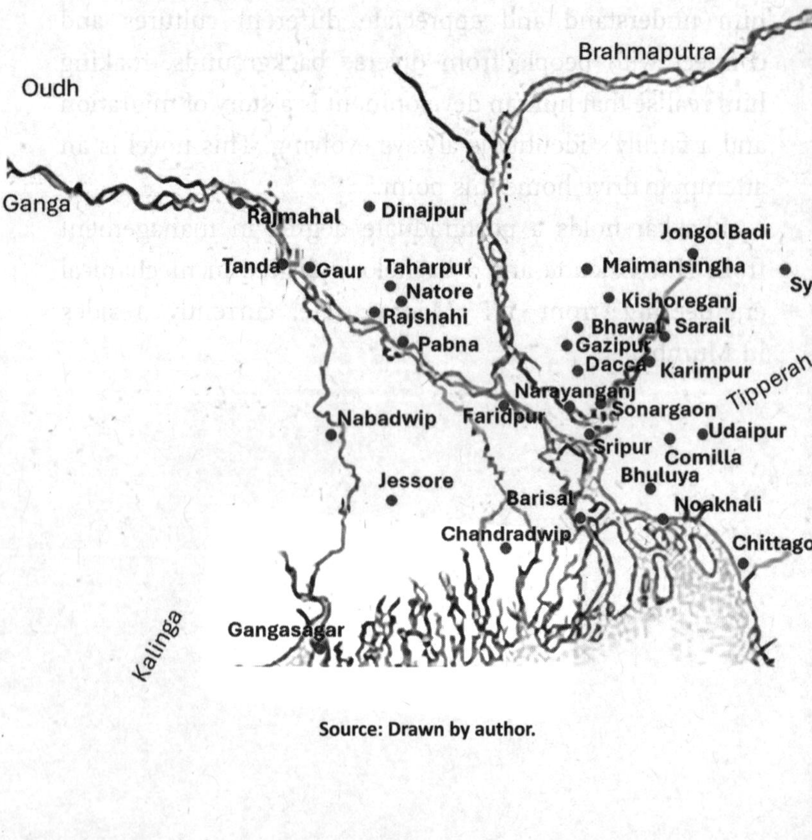

Source: Drawn by author.

THE RAJA OF JONGOL BADI

A TALE OF LOVE AND REBELLION

BHASKAR SOM

Om Books International

First published in 2025 by

Om Books International

Corporate & Editorial Office
A-12, Sector 64, Noida 201 301
Uttar Pradesh, India
Phone: +91 120 477 4100
Email: editorial@ombooks.com
Website: www.ombooksinternational.com

Sales Office
107, Ansari Road, Darya Ganj,
New Delhi 110 002, India
Phone: +91 11 4000 9000
Email: sales@ombooks.com
Website: www.ombooks.com

ISBN: 978-81-19750-97-9

Printed in India

To

my late grandfather Samarendra Nath Som

Contents

Preface

When I was a toddler, I used to hear with fascination my grandfather's tales of the golden land that was East Bengal (now Bangladesh) and from where he hailed. The names like Buri Ganga, Sadarbazaar, Shitalakshya, Ramna Kalibadi, Sonargaon, Goalundo Ghat are still etched in my memory. Although I was born and brought up in West Bengal, it is Bangladesh, the land of my forefathers, that has always fascinated and intrigued me. I have therefore been reading about the evolution of Bengalis—particularly the ones typically derided as Bangals—from my college days.

The cultural traditions of the indigenous population of Bengal are distinct from that of the dominant civilisation of north India. The renowned historian, late Hara Prasad Sastri—best known for discovering the Charyapada, the earliest known examples of Bengali literature—made the following observation, "When the Aryans reached Punjab, Bengal had already attained a high level of civilisation, and when they had advanced up to Allahabad, they had begun to abuse Bengalis as speechless and devoid of religious sense, presumably, being jealous of their distinctive culture."

Not surprisingly, the early Aryans referred to Bengal as the land of the *asuras* (demons).

The uniqueness of Bengal's cultural and historical background lies in the fact that it is pre-Vedic and non-Vedic. The Bengali society at the dawn of Buddhism (around fifth century BC) was agricultural and casteless unlike the Aryans who were pastoral and had a Chaturvarnashram stratification. Heterodoxy prevailed across Bengal along with tantrism. When Buddhism spread in the east, Bengalis embraced it in large numbers but transformed it into a kind of Tantric Buddhism. Jainism too had considerable influence in Bengal. Brahminism is believed to have entered Bengal under Adisura around AD 800, though it blossomed under the Sena dynasty in the twelfth century. The caste system was vigorously pursued from that time although the less privileged Bengalis revolted by converting to Islam or Chaitanya Mahaprabhu's Vaishnavism.

Bengal, before the advent of the Britishers, was referred to by its various territorial regions. The Britishers coined the term Bengal, borrowing it from the Portuguese who called the region Shahi Bangalah or Imperial Bengal. Blessed by natural resources, Bengal prospered during the medieval period. When Hiuen Tsang visited the present-day Murshidabad in the seventh century AD, he described the wealth of Bengal in glowing terms. He commented that the country was well inhabited and abundant in fruits and flowers, and the people were rich, friendly and patrons of learning.

Notwithstanding Bengal's prosperity, her people—protected by the elaborate riverine network—neglected combative skills. The peace and prosperity of Bengal were shattered in the early thirteenth century when the Turko-Afghan military general Bakhtiyar Khilji rode into the Bengal's ancient capital Lakhnauti (later renamed Gaur). So swift had been his advance that only eighteen of his riders had been able to keep up with him. Legend has it that the townspeople mistook Khilji and his men for traders and the alarm was only raised when they drew their swords and started slaughtering the guards inside Lakshmana Sena's palace. On hearing about Khilji's arrival, the octogenarian king Lakshmana Sena—who had just sat down for lunch—fled barefoot to faraway Bikrampur (in modern-day Bangladesh). From then, Bengal was primarily ruled by governors of the Delhi Sultanate, though there were some independent reigns too, most notable was that of Hussain Shahi dynasty in the early sixteenth century.

Just as it appeared that Bengal was regaining her lost glory under the Hussain Shahi dynasty, the Mughals captured Delhi and proceeded to capture Bengal—the granary of the Delhi Sultanate. Meanwhile, the Mrauk U kingdom rose to power in adjacent Burma (modern-day Myanmar) and frequently raided south-eastern Bengal, while the Portuguese who controlled trade over the Bay of Bengal set up a trading centre around modern-day Chittagong to ensure a steady supply of rice and textiles and plunder the rich hinterland.

As the Afghans, Mughals, Arakanese and the Portuguese pillaged the economic heartland of Bengal, a group of important landlords aligned their forces to stop the plundering and protect the wealth of Bengal. While it is believed there were more than twelve landlords who came together, they are commonly referred to as Baro Bhuiyans (*bhuiyan* is derived from the Sanskrit word *bhumi*), or twelve landlords who were more like soldier-landlords. The *Maimansingha Gitika* by Rai Bahadur Dinesh Chandra Sen eulogises their heroic tales and it is commonly believed that Isa Khan (popularly known as Isha Khan in Bengal) was the leader of this resistance force. The Gitika carries many anecdotes about Isa, right from how his father—a devout Hindu—converted to Islam, his valour against the Mughals, how his in-laws persecuted his family when he was no more and how his grandchild again rose to gain dominance over the Bhati region.

My story, loosely based on Raja Isa Khan, recollects the power struggles in sixteenth-century Bengal while recounting the love story between Isa and Sona, the daughter of another prominent bhuiyan. There are controversies regarding Isa's origins. However, Abul Fazl in *Ain-i-Akbari*, considered to be the most authentic source of information on Isa, clearly states that his father Sulaiman Khan was killed by Taj Khan Karrani, the founder of the Karrani dynasty (the last dynasty to rule the Sultanate of Bengal), and Isa and his brother Ismail were captured and sold as slaves.

There are controversies too regarding Isa's mother and speculation prevails on the identity of the princess whom Sulaiman married. History is often distorted to create legends and myths, and it is therefore important to check the chronological order of events to separate fact from fiction.

Rai Bahadur Dinesh Chandra Sen in his book *Eastern Bengal Ballads* (the English edition of the Gitika) has argued that Sulaiman's wife Syeda was Ghiyasuddin Mahmud Shahi's daughter. I concur with him.

Nevertheless, whatever be the controversies surrounding Isa Khan, he is remembered in the ballads as a benevolent ruler, one who made enormous sacrifices for his people.

While every attempt has been made to maintain the historical facts, certain episodes—like the romance between Isa and Princess Pari—have been imagined. My objective is to both entertain and educate. The book is an endeavour to bring to life interesting characters and events of a bygone era, and is an ode to the millions of Bengalis with a rich cultural history.

I hope you enjoy reading the book as much as I enjoyed writing it.

Prologue

*T*HIS ISA IS A REAL *pain in the neck. Unless I quickly bring him under control, the collective strength of these Bengali chieftains will expand rapidly. I thought Maharana Pratap of Mewar was my biggest thorn, but now it looks Isa Khan is my biggest worry.*

As the thoughts raged through Emperor Akbar's mind, he hardly realised that he had barged into his favourite wife Mariam's room.

It was the autumn of 1584. The scorching heat of the summer was behind, as was the sticky humidity of the monsoon. Within a few days, the neighbourhood would erupt to the vibrant festivities of Diwali, lighting up in a burst of colours and sounds. While the crème de la crème looked forward to the royal banquet, the commoners awaited the generosity of the emperor. Everyone eagerly looked forward to the upcoming celebrations except the person whose religious tolerance had made Diwali such a popular festival in the capital city of Agra. Abu'l-Fath Jalal-ud-Din Muhammad Akbar had reasons to be a worried man.

It was almost three decades since Akbar had ascended the throne at the tender age of thirteen. He had understood early in life that territorial expansion would not only increase the security of his kingdom, but also boost its economic power by providing access to more resources, such as fertile land, minerals, trade routes and strategic locations. Akbar could look back with pride on how he had consolidated his power in India by subjugating his formidable adversaries—the fiercely independent Rajputs—through both military and diplomatic approaches.

Akbar recollected the discussions he had with his commander Bairam Khan as they marched towards Delhi after the Second Battle of Panipat way back in 1556. This had followed barely after a year of the Battle of Sirhind in which Emperor Humayun's troops had destroyed Sikandar Shah Suri's army.

"Khan-i-Khanan, how come the enemy was able to regroup so quickly, albeit under their Hindu commander Hemu, and capture Delhi the moment Abbu died?"

Bairam's words still resonated with Akbar.

"*Mian,* the capital of Delhi is financed by the granary of the east. By the time your father understood the same, Sher Shah had seized suzerainty of Bengal. With the funds available at his disposal, Sher Shah could buy as many mercenary soldiers as needed. Meanwhile, your father's finances dwindled and he was not able to pay his soldiers on time, which left his army disgruntled. Hence, his position weakened. You need to have control of Bengal for your revenues which will help you in funding your military missions. Just imagine the kind of wealth Bengal gives access to which enabled the Suris to regroup so quickly. The ride to Delhi starts from Bengal!"

Akbar reflected, *Bengal needs to be totally controlled at the earliest ...*

"What's troubling you, my beloved Jalal-ud-Din?"

Mariam-uz-Zamani was surprised at the unexpected visit as the emperor usually presided over his court during this time. Born Harkha Bai to Raja Bharmal of Amber, Mariam had married Akbar when both were twenty years old, and over the years she had come to know the shahenshah so well that she could now read him like the back of her hand. She was also the mother of Akbar's eldest son and the heir apparent, Prince Salim.

Mariam looked up at the emperor, as he approached her divan, dragging his leg left slightly. Excessive horse riding in his childhood had left his limbs somewhat bowed inwards. Mariam loved gazing at his eyes but today, the spark was missing from them. Mariam could make out Akbar was disconcerted.

What worried Akbar was uprisings in Bengal. Conquering the Rajputana territories in the western part of his empire had a heavy toll on his exchequer. Ordinarily, these would have been financed by revenue collections from Bengal, but there was disquiet in the far eastern territory of his regime. The revenue slowdown in Bengal for the Mughals was aiding the local landlords there and making them stronger. Akbar knew he had to send troops immediately so that the rebels could be vanquished before the monsoon sets in, else his army could face the same fate as his last governor Shahbaz Khan's army.

"Shahbaz Khan has failed in his mission to capture Bengal and has now returned to Fatehpur Sikri. Over the last few years, I have sent so many governors to Bengal—Khan Jahan, Muzaffar Khan Turbati, Mirza Aziz and now Shahbaz Khan—but all of them have failed to rein in the rebels. All these subahdars complained of a group of twelve Bengali zamindars called Baro Bhuiyans who have become too powerful and rebellious, but their chief grouse is against Isa Khan. I am at a loss what to do now!"

The beautiful Mariam wickedly grinned.

"Aren't you thankful to the Rajputs for providing you so many beautiful ladies like me? Why, even two of your Navratnas are Rajputs—Raja Man Singh and Raja Todar Mal."

"Mariam, you know you are my favourite. Yes, I was barely twenty years old when I was campaigning all the time in Rajputana. Thankfully, I learnt early on during my first campaign against Rana Pratap of Mewar that controlling Rajputana through outright subjugation could be difficult. Hence, I have subsequently followed a policy of integration through diplomacy, alliances and strategic marriages. But, what is your point, Mariam?"

"What is there to think about? Send your precious Navaratna to Bengal with a large battalion. My *bhatija* has successfully governed Kabul and decimated Afghan rebels there in the past now let him go eastwards and destroy the local resistance there."

"You are so right, Begum! I will immediately ask Man Singh to proceed towards Bengal. Isa Khan, your end is near!"

1

Kalidas Gajdani Embraces Love and Creates Destiny

AD 1534

EVERY DAY BEFORE SUNRISE, KALIDAS Singh would take a dip in the Ganga, be it summer, monsoon or winter. Today was no different. He took his bath, changed into a spotless white dhoti-kurta, picked up a pail of water and headed towards the Shiva temple near Jahaj Ghat, the site of an ancient port of Gaur. Kalidas, a devotee of Mahadeva, would visit the temple daily at dawn and dusk to pray. On amavasya every month, he would present gold-plated elephant souvenirs to the first twelve Brahmin pandits he met. This is how he earned his sobriquet Kalidas Gajdani—the gifter of elephants—though the townsfolk were puzzled by his staunch Shaivism in a place where most Hindus worshipped Goddess Tara or Lord Vishnu.

While native Bengalis mostly worshipped the goddess, Kalidas worshipped Lord Shiva as he was not from Gaur originally. He was born in Oudh (modern-day central Uttar Pradesh) and belonged to the powerful and wealthy Baishwara Kshatriya Rajput community who were devout Shaivites. This ancient Hindu warrior caste's original home was in the Deccan, and they migrated to Oudh in the mid-thirteenth century.

Kalidas's grandfather, Dhanapat Singh—the ruler of Oudh—had constructed several temples dedicated to the god in his kingdom. His son Bhagirath—being the scholarly kind—got unsettled by the growing violence in northern India and had shifted to tranquil Gaur during Nasiruddin Nusrat Shah's regime and was now employed as the diwan of Ghiyasuddin Mahmud Shah, last sultan of the illustrious Hussain Shahi dynasty.

The tall and well-built Kalidas appeared to tower over the shivling as he entered the place of worship. Yet, as he gently sat down, cleaned the idol with *gangajal*, smeared *bhasma* on the *lingam* and lit the diya, one could feel his deep devotion to the lord. At that time, Bengalis commonly believed that only dacoits were ardent worshippers of Neelkantha, but Kalidas, despite his black hair, brown eyes and thick moustache, could not be mistaken for one. His fair complexion and chiselled looks screamed out nobility.

"*Om Namah Shivaya, Om Namah Shivaya, Om Namah Shivaya* ..." Kalidas's sonorous voice echoed through the sanctum.

It was a sight to see him pray.

Today, after finishing his prayers, Kalidas rushed home as dark monsoon clouds loomed over the city. He loved the rains and did not mind getting wet, but he knew the spatter from the puddles would stain his starched white dhoti and removing the marks would be a pain. He quickened his pace. As he scurried home, the devotees from the adjacent Ramkeli temple broke out into a song "*Hare Krishna, Hare Krishna, Krishna Krishna, Hare Hare, Hare Rama, Hare Rama, Rama Rama, Hare Hare.*"

The temple was built on the site where Sri Chaitanya Mahaprabhu had once resided for a few days on his journey to Brindavan. The land at Ramkeli belonged to the brothers, Rup and Sanatan, the two great disciples of Sri Chaitanya Mahaprabhu. The brothers were so inspired by the spiritual lessons of Sri Chaitanya Mahaprabhu that they became his greatest disciples and renounced their life of luxury to spread the message of Lord Krishna.

Kalidas felt that Chaitanya calling himself Gaurhari and identifying himself as the Vishnu of Gaur were a sacrilege. He also detested the fact that the Muslims and the Untouchables could be indoctrinated into Vaishnavism. Shutting his ears with his palms, he almost broke into a run to escape the kirtan.

As he neared the Bodo Sona Masjid, Kalidas looked up to admire its turrets. The gigantic mosque, with its eleven entrances and forty-four gilded domes, never failed to fascinate Kalidas. He loved watching the kaleidoscopic reflections of the morning sunrise on the masjid's rooftop, although today, the downcast sky gave a sombre look to the mosque.

"*Allahu Akbar*! *Allahu Akbar*!"

As he stood their admiring the mosque, the cries rang through the air. The morning namaz had just ended.

Kalidas smiled to himself, admiring the cosmopolitan culture where the natives peacefully coexisted with the Afghans, Arabs, Portuguese, Chinese and Burmese. He wondered whether there was any other region where various sects could live in harmony while practising their individual religions and beliefs.

Kalidas was now near the Dakhil Darwaza, the impressive 109-year-old entrance to the fortified city of Gaur. Kalidas considered Gaur the most beautiful city although he would be the first to admit that he had not seen many cities. He knew that successive empires, starting from the Palas to the Senas down to the current Hussain Shahi dynasty, all had played important roles in making Gaur the city it was today. Kalidas would have been scandalised if anyone had suggested to him a couple of years back that he would be settling outside Oudh in Gaur.

How times change. My purvaj Raja Harshvardhan of Thaneshwar was a bitter rival of King Shashanka of Bengal. They repeatedly waged war against each other. Yet today, Pitaji is a diwan to the king in this rival kingdom. If only they had conquered it, I would have been the king of this kingdom. Gaur was then known as Karna Suvarna ... Kalidas smiled as he recollected how the earlier name changed to Gaur a corruption of the word gur. *Bengalis and their sweet tooth*!

The guardsmen bowed when Kalidas entered through the Dakhil Darwaza, the northern entrance to the emperor's durbar, his palace, the harem, servant quarters, the royal prison and residence of a few court officials. Twelve towers mounted with guns stood around the Dakhil Darwaza and guns fired when distinguished visitors or the emperor entered, hence the entrance was also called the Salami Darwaza.

The lesser privileged entered through the Kotwali Darwaza at the southern end of the palace grounds. The arch was about fifty feet high and the wall was very thick. One had to pass eight more gates before reaching the sultan's durbar.

The Dakhil Darwaza had been renovated during Hussain Shah rule and its impressive facade with a stucco finish and beautiful terracotta carvings on the porch reminded Kalidas of the successful amalgamation of Hindu and Islamic architecture in Bengal. The entrance, made of red bricks and around sixty feet tall, was square in shape, with each side equal to almost ninety feet. There were four towers at the corners, while inside the Darwaza, the overwhelming arches were supported by black granite piers.

A seventy-five-feet tall wall encircled the entire complex, which apart from various buildings, monuments and mausoleums, also contained several beautiful lakes, manicured gardens and orchards. Seeing that rain was imminent, Kalidas wanted to cut through the garden, but he saw Sultan Ghiyasuddin playing polo with a few other nobles on the green lawns. He realised it would be prudent to take the circuitous paved road and stay off the grass. He had just crossed the palace walls when the sky opened. Kalidas started running towards his quarters.

Near the palace walls, atop Gumti Darwaza, stood Syeda Momena Khatu. Usually, the womenfolk came escorted when visiting the gates, but Syeda was an exception. She did as she pleased. The young, vivacious and attractive Syeda, with her big round eyes and sharp features, was the youngest and favourite daughter of Ghiyasuddin. When she heard about her father playing polo, she climbed up to the higher floors of the darwaza to not only enjoy the game and the cool breeze, but also to keep an eye on her beloved who was expected anytime now. And there he was!

As Syeda saw Kalidas dart across to his residence, her heart throbbed wildly and she thought to herself, *I have to meet him now.*

Syeda had proposed to Kalidas a few weeks ago, but Kalidas had turned down her proposal on religious grounds. *How do I win him over? I must tell him the truth ...*

She quickly climbed down from the Gumti Darwaza and dashed to her chamber, not minding the rain one bit.

"Manda! Manda! Come immediately!"

Her trusted maid rushed instantly with a worried expression on her face.

"What happened, Syeda didi?"

Syeda broke into a smile on seeing Manda.

Syeda playfully pinched Manda's cheeks and hurriedly asked, "Manda, have you managed to cook those samosas for Kalidas as I had instructed?"

Manda winked and answered, "Dada babu really relished them and have been insisting that I prepare them again for his evening tea."

Syeda burst out laughing.

"My dear Manda, can you please prepare some of those samosas for me now?"

Syeda quickly put the fritters in a bell metal bowl, covered it with banana leaves and sprinted to Bhagirath's residence. *I have to meet Kalidas alone*! She knew his father was in the durbar. The house would be empty now except for Kalidas, as his mother and siblings were still in Oudh. They were expected in the next few weeks.

All houses within the fortified citadel were single-storeyed and made of red bricks. This gave the town the impression of a red city. As Syeda stepped into the courtyard of Bhagirath's house, she noted peacock feathers hanging from the wall and the terracotta tiles on the floor.

"Kali! Kali! Come out please!"

Kalidas, who had just changed into a fresh set of clothes, stepped out into the courtyard. His heart skipped a beat on seeing the beautiful Syeda in front of him. His heart broke when he had to reject her marriage proposal, but he had no choice—his father would never agree to this matrimonial alliance.

Letting out a sigh, he gently asked, "Shehzadi, why have you come here? Have I not told you in no uncertain words that we are two straight lines, you a Muslim and I a Hindu, and that the two lines can never meet?"

"Yes, yes, I remember that!"

Syeda rolled her eyes.

"But I doubt whether you are a Hindu any more."

"What do you mean? How dare you ..."

"Shhhh. Here, eat your favourite snack before answering that!"

Kalidas was puzzled.

Syeda held up the bowl in front of Kalidas and asked, "Kali, do they look familiar?"

Kalidas grinned.

"Yes! Has Manda cooked them? These *batata* fries are really tasty! Thank God to the Portuguese for popularising these in Gaur!"

Syeda shook her head and started sniggering.

"Kali, you may be a great scholar, but you are sooo ignorant of the ways of the world. This is not potato, but minced beef and vegetables.

She cackled seeing Kalidas's shocked expression.

"Yes, you heard that right young man! You have eaten beef. You are no longer a Hindu! Did you believe you could scorn the advances of a woman so easily on religious grounds? Now convert to Islam and marry me! I know you want to!"

He screamed, "Shehzadi, what have you done? You have tricked me into eating beef! I have lost my religion! There is no way I can live any more. It is best for me to die!"

Kalidas madly bolted towards the Dakhil Darwaza to drown in the Ganga. Syeda ran after him. Sultan Ghiyasuddin had just changed into his imperial dress and was walking towards his court when he spotted a distraught Kalidas. He immediately asked his bodyguards, "*Roko usko*! Stop him! And bring him to me!

Kalidas was soon produced before him.

"You seem perturbed, my boy! What's the matter?"

Kalidas blurted out, "Thanks to the princess, I have eaten beef. I have lost my religion and can only die now!"

Ghiyasuddin glanced at Syeda. He was aware of her feelings towards Kalidas. Syeda never hid anything from her father.

"Syeda, what is he talking about?"

"Abbu, he is right! I fed him beef samosas on the sly. How dare he refuse my ..."

Syeda stood there with arms akimbo.

"*Khamosh*!"

He knew Syeda was just like him and never gave up on ambitions. He had to kill his nephew to ascend the throne.

"I am so sorry to hear about your predicament, Kalidas. What Syeda has done is deplorable! But let us seek the advice of Diwanji."

Thus, Bhagirath was summoned. He came and joined Sultan Ghiyasuddin, Syeda and Kalidas in the emperor's private chamber. The sultan appraised Bhagirath of the developments and then added, "I have no son and only two daughters. Only my eldest and youngest daughters are alive. The middle one died long ago. My elder daughter is married to a pir and he is simply not interested in running the kingdom. But Kalidas comes from a long line of illustrious warriors and if he marries Syeda, he will become the emperor once I die. Please ask your son to marry Syeda and become the heir apparent."

To accept the sultan's offer would be a terrible blow to Bhagirath's religion. And, if he failed to assuage Kalidas's fears, he could risk losing his son.

Bhagirath's shoulders drooped, and he let out a long sigh.

He slowly turned to Kalidas and hesitantly said, "What is done is done, Kali.You are a follower of the Mahadeva. Mahadeva does not discriminate between the origins of his worshippers. He looks at a Brahmin and at an Untouchable through the same lens. What the sultan therefore says makes sense. I implore you to marry the princess."

Kalidas was intrigued.

What is the sultan and Babuji propositioning? My purvajs could never succeed in vanquishing Bengal. Yet, through a subterfuge of a Bengali princess, I could now become the ruler of Bengal and accomplish the long-cherished dream of my ancestors. This is a golden opportunity ...

He reached out for Syeda's hand and announced, "*Mujhe yeh rishta qubool hai*!"

Syeda squealed in delight.

Thus, at the Qadam Rasul Masjid—where Sultan Nusrat Shah had enshrined a stone reproduction of an impression of the Prophet's foot—the wedding between Kalidas and Syeda was solemnised. Kalidas Singh Gajdani became Sulaiman Khan. Within a few years, the couple was blessed with a son Isa Khan.

But Kalidas's dream of ascending the throne was shattered when Sher Shah Suri attacked Gaur in 1537. Sultan Ghiyasuddin's army capitulated in front of the onslaught and the emperor escaped to south Bengal. Sulaiman and Syeda fled to Sarail in Bhati (in modern-day Bangladesh) with young Isa in tow to start their life afresh. Alas, their misery had just begun!

2

The Begum and the Ghulam

AD 1563

IT WAS MID-AUGUST. DUSK WAS settling over the mountainous town of Qazvin. The horizon was splashed with a brilliant lustre of yellow, orange and red. Sunsets made Isa nostalgic. It reminded him of his idyllic childhood back home in Sarail where the Meghna River reflected every fleeting shade of amber, red, purple, orange and gold during sunset. To overcome the disquietude in this distant land, Isa would typically spend the long, cold evenings at the Sa'd al-Saltaneh caravanserai with his brother Ismail and other mates of the Safavid army. There, they took turns at smoking the hookah, drinking a few rounds of arak and gorging on bread, kebabs, pistachios and pomegranates amidst the Arab, Black, Pathan, Chinese and Mongol customers. The tipsy soldiers would stumble back to their tents on Cepah Street at midnight when the serai closed.

But today was Ashura, the tenth day of Muharram. It was a day for mourning the martyrdom of the Prophet's grandson Hussain. This was the day for praying, doing charity and fasting for every Mussalman in the town to purify their soul and destroy all the sins of the previous year.

Now, as dusk was settling, it was time to congregate for the Maghrib prayer and then break the fast with one's near ones. Ismail was Isa's only family in Qazvin, but Isa wanted to break his fast with someone else. So, as they proceeded towards the mosque, Isa feigned indigestion and told his brother, "Bhai, I am not feeling well and plan to retire to the tent after the namaz. You all please continue to the serai."

Ismail should have been concerned, but he had noticed Isa skipping meals on important dates a few times over the last couple of years. He remained silent. Ismail was aware something was amiss. On such occasions, when Ismail returned in the night and peeped into his brother's tent, Isa would be absent. Whenever Ismail had quizzed Isa about it, Isa's response had always been that he had gone outdoors "to answer nature's call". He would lovingly call Isa *pet patla* behind his back, although he never dared to do so in his presence.

Ismail, like the other soldiers, was in awe of his tall, well-built elder brother, who apart from being strong and courageous, was also an excellent swordsman. Ismail had never seen Isa come out worsted in a fight. He was secretly grateful that he had his brother as his friend, protector and guide in this distant kingdom of Turan, where both were employed as *ghulams* in Shah Tahmasp's army.

As Isa trudged towards the tent, his mind flashed back to that summer of 1554 when he saw Taj Khan Karrani, an army general in Sher Shah Suri's army approach their mansion. News had spread that Taj Khan had beheaded their father Sulaiman Khan, who had declared his independence at Sarail, on the battlefield.

"Quick Ismail, *bhago*! Run for your life!" Isa had implored his brother.

"*Nahin*! Let them come!"

An adamant and proud Ismail barely in his teens refused to budge.

While Isa was a much married man. Isa's eyes welled up as he remembered his *ammi* fall at the feet of Taj Khan, begging him to spare her sons. However, the impenitent Taj Khan captured the brothers and took them as slaves. Even today, Isa would shudder every time he remembered his ammi lie crumpled on the ground while Ismail and he were dragged away.

Isa stopped and looked back. As far as he could discern, no one had followed him. He had good soldier's instinct. He quickly made his way towards the Meimoon Ghal'eh, the ruined castle that lay just outside the town. On his right lay the walled garden quarters where Shah Tahmasp resided, and he could see the faint silhouette of Kolah Farangi where Pari stayed. He wished he was visiting her there instead of trekking up to the Meimoon Ghal'eh.

He knew even thinking about Pari was haram and he would be beheaded if he were seen anywhere near the princess. He also believed their relationship had no future and he was just a tool of gratification for the princess. *But I am a living corpse anyway, so I might as well enjoy the few moments of recklessness and pleasure, and from death will come freedom. Freedom from slavery, freedom from bondage, freedom from ennui and freedom from the cruel twists of fate.*

The life of a slave soldier in the peaceful Safavid regime was rather excrutiatingly boring. Isa looked for excitement and passion. When he had finally persuaded Sikandar Shah Suri to allow both Ismail and him to join the army, he had hoped the battlefield would provide him the necessary resuscitation from the life of a sex slave in the Afghan army, where beardless, adolescent boys were victims of adult men's desire. But the Suri army lost to the Mughals at the Battle of Sirhind, and Isa and Ismail were sent as presents to Shah Tahmasp I of Persia, who had given shelter to Emperor Humayun during his exile.

On their way to Turan, Isa gathered that the Ottomans and Uzbeks frequently attacked the Safavid kingdom and he and Ismail could demonstrate their valour in the Safavid army. However, by the time they arrived at Qazvin, the shah had signed the peace treaty of Amasya with the Ottoman Empire and peace reigned in the kingdom.

As the Safavid Empire enjoyed harmony under the new treaty, a bored Isa started drowning himself in arak. *What is a soldier without a fight?*

One day, as he lay sozzled at the serai, he regaled Ismail and fellow companions with a couplet by Omar Khayyam, "Here's to the man who owns the land that bears the grapes that makes the wine that tastes as good as this does."

The shah was informed about this incident through his network of spies and a bemused emperor summoned Isa to his court.

Isa had heard from his ammi tales of the splendid court of his grandfather Sultan Ghiyasuddin, but he had never experienced such grandeur before. Marvelling at the intricate calligraphy and the exquisite carpets, Isa turned his gaze to the bearded shah sitting on a jewel-clad divan, resplendent in a white turban embroidered with pearls.

The shah glanced at Isa and absorbed his great physique, his aquiline features, his trimmed-bearded handsome face, the grey penetrating eyes, the blue sarband matched with his blue salwar complemented by a white *jameh* and grey *jubba*, and the confident gait.

"Young man, tell me about yourself."

Isa bowed and replied, "Shahenshah, my brother and I are your ghulams; we are your presents from Badshah Humayun. I am a trained swordsman. And I also happen to be well versed in Urdu and Farsi."

The Shah's ears perked up. He was a leading patron of arts and literature and was pleasantly surprised to see a kindred spirit. Isa could make a suitable instructor to his younger son.

The shah chuckled and asked, "Are you a Sunni like the rascal Humayun?"

"*Huzoor*, your religion is my religion."

Shah Tahmasp was delighted.

The shah shifted his gaze to the seven men wearing red turbans and yellow kurtas and said, "These are my Kizilbash, the leaders of my tribesmen, what you in Hindustan call *senapatis*. They have been instructing my children in the art of warfare, but I want you to teach Urdu to my younger son, Prince Suleiman Mirza."

"Shahnama-yi Shahi, your wish is my command."

But even as Isa spoke, his eyes took in the disconcerted looks of the Kizilbash commanders. But what really attracted his attention was the petite veiled maiden sitting behind the shah.

"*Who is she*?" Isa thought.

He was surprised to see a lady in the court, for he always thought that women were supposed to stay inside the *zenana*. But over the next few years, as he taught Shahzadeh Suleiman the fine art of warfare and Urdu and regaled him with stories of betrayal and treachery from the Bengal Sultanate, he came to understand the functioning of courts better. He realised that women could not only be present in courts, but also be elevated to prominent positions based on their lineage and influence. And he learnt that the veiled beauty was Pari Khan Khanum, the second and favourite daughter of Shah Tahmasp.

In many of his sessions with the prince, Isa often sensed the presence of a third person behind the curtain of the camp set up for the prince's training. One day, Isa adroitly placed himself to peep behind the purdah, and found himself staring into the bewitching black almond-shaped eyes of Pari.

Princess Pari, without losing a beat, said, "Isa, your tales from Bengal are so fascinating. And what you are imparting to my brother here is an absolute masterpiece of political manoeuvres. I would love to see your land. You know, Ibn

Batuta had said he had seen no country where provisions were cheaper! I have also heard it is one of the most prosperous regions in the world."

Isa was immensely impressed that a girl in distant Qazvin, situated over one thousand kilometres from his homeland, knew so much about his beloved homeland.

Thus sprang a friendship between a begum and a former slave, fuelled by passionate love for poetry, politics and each other.

Pari too was married, but her *mian* Prince Badi-al Zaman Mirza Safavi was the governor of Sistan and lived 1,300 kilometres from Qazvin. His long absences from Qazvin gave the lovebirds ample time to spend with each other. The more time Isa spent with Pari, the more he fell in love with her extensive knowledge, strong will, free spirit, quiet strength and smashing looks.

This is no ordinary girl. I am lucky to be in her company. This is all I need in my woman, something I could never find in Fatima ...

Isa smiled, reminiscing about their numerous encounters over the last five years. He remembered Pari's quizzical look when he told the prince that his father too was named Sulaiman like him. Pari had several times asked him about his father, but he never divulged his antecedents to anyone in a foreign land. One could never trust anyone when in exile. Not even Pari.

Whether it was his opinion about the threat from the Uzbeks from the east or the need for more caravanserais on the Silk Route to benefit the carpet trade, he had Pari's rapt attention.

"Pari, do you know that back home the natives hate the strength of the Uzbeks so much that they have started using the word *ujbuk* for fools?"

Pari's eyes glimmered as she smiled, "Like *barbar* in Arabic!"

Isa's heart still missed a beat whenever he reminisced about that afternoon over two years ago, when they challenged each other to recite their favourite couplets simultaneously. Both looked into each other's eyes and without missing a beat quoted Amir Khusrau, "*Mun tu shudam tu mun shudi, mun tu shudam tu jaan shudi. Taakas na guyad baad azeen, mun deegaram tu deegari* (I have become you, and you have become me, I am the body, you the soul, so that no one can say, hereafter, that you are someone else and I am someone else)."

Neither of them fluttered an eyelid while reciting, and Isa wished he could continue to stare into her big black eyes with long eyelashes. Then Pari, feeling a bit embarrassed, ran inside, though shortly afterwards, she came out to shyly hand him a note which read: "From today, you are my *isk*," with her lip mark embossed on it.

"Isk as in *ishq*?"

Isa tried hard to keep a straight face.

Pari winked at him.

"Isk is short for Isa Khan."

And with that Pari swiftly turned and vanished behind the purdah.

But Isa was sure he caught a naughty smile on her lips.

Isa looked at the sky. The resplendent moon was four days from her full glory, as if smiling at the world on this holy day. But its full view was blocked by the silhouette of the Meimoon Ghal'eh. Isa had been so preoccupied thinking about his past and Pari that he did not realise that he was at the base of the castle. He carefully trekked up to the ruins.

Located right in the middle of the city of Qazvin, Meimoon Ghal'eh never ceased to fascinate Isa. Now in ruins, the castle covered an area of over six acres and must have been an impressive military fortress during its prime. The dome had collapsed and the eight towers surrounding the castle had also crumpled, but Isa had found remnants of a few hidden tunnels underneath the labyrinth and had named the one behind the entrance as their meeting point.

"We will call it Parinama."

"So is it in the name of Pari or transforming Pari?"

"You know Sanskrit also?"

This woman never ceased to amaze him.

"There is a lot you need to find out about me!"

Isa had now reached Parinama. He looked down towards the town where merriment was continuing, and people could still be seen on the streets. He knew this was going to be a long night as Pari had to be discreet and not be caught loitering on the streets. Political power played out among the Kizilbash, the zenana and the Shah's harem, and Pari had to perform a perfect balancing act between these various factions. Further, today being Ashura, she had to celebrate the occasion with her family members to ensure she continued to have their trust. Isa sensed Pari had stayed back in Qazvin after her betrothal to strengthen her position in the regime and rule the Safavid kingdom once Shah Tahmasp was no more.

Isa was now tired and hungry. He sat down on the ground, resting his back on a collapsed tower, waiting for Pari to arrive. He looked up at the sky, searched for the Saptarishi and traced its two pointer stars to Dhruva Tara or the Pole Star. He gathered it was now four hours after sunset. His *abbujan* had taught him to correctly predict time when he was a kid. Lying on the ground, staring at the sky and recollecting the bygone days, he thought about his ammi and bibi. He hoped they were fine, neither of them enslaved nor living in a brothel. He was stuck in a loveless marriage with Fatima but held her in great affection as they grew up together as cousins. As he waited for the princess to arrive, Isa drifted to sleep.

3

The Secret Rendezvous

I HOPE ISA HAS NOT *returned to his tent. He can get bored so easily*, thought Pari as she tried to mingle with the crowd. Everyone was enjoying themselves thoroughly. All were busy eating and talking animatedly. The spread was elaborate, with over one thousand dishes laid out for supper. Pari was at the Ali Qapu palace, with her father and his consorts and children, including the chief queen, Sultanum Begum. But her mind was somewhere else. Seeing her father busy romancing her mother and his favourite wife—the beautiful Sultan-Agha Khanum, made Pari feel miserable and lonely.

She kept sipping her watermelon juice and eyeing the succulent kebabs and almost felt tempted to have one. But she stopped and chided herself,

This would not be fair! I can't partake of food while Isa is waiting for me. We have pledged to break our fast together.

She called out to her khansama, "Ikram, *jaldi aao*. Pack a dinner box with the tastiest kebabs and naans, and a bottle of madeira!"

It was over six years ago that she was betrothed to Prince Badi-al Zaman her cousin, who was several years older to her. Her father had adopted Badi-al as his son and appointed him as the governor of Sistan. The thought of being wedded to a man for whom she had sisterly feelings, revolted Pari. She did not want to lead the life of her stepmom, Sultanum Begum, who despite being the first wife and the maternal first cousin of her father was ignored by him. Worse, the begum's favourite son Ismail was imprisoned by the shah because a courtier had convinced the emperor that Ismail was planning to overthrow him. Pari was sure her ammi had a role to play behind the incarceration.

Pari was aware that it was unusual for a woman to be a ruler in Islamic society. But had not Razia Sultana become the sultan of Delhi almost three centuries ago? Like Iltutmish, who had founded the Delhi Sultanate, her father Shah Tahmasp had established the Safavid dynasty. Razia was Iltutmish's favourite daughter, and she was her father's apple of the eye. The parallels were too many. Ever since she had read about Razia Sultana and her travails, she harboured ambitions to succeed her father.

She had reflected on this with Badi-al after their nikah.

"You are aware how deep-rooted the politics is in our empire and how fleeting one's position can be in the hierarchy. Most insinuations typically originate in the zenana and hence it is important to keep one's ear to the ground. Jaan, please I need to stay back here to keep tab on all developments. This will ensure we are in the emperor's good books."

Badi-al welcomed her suggestion. After all, it would be easier for him to continue with his indiscretions if the Shah's favourite daughter was not living with him.

She knew there were rumours that she was having an illicit relationship with her father. The shah trusted her and valued her guidance, for the menfolk in the empire were either overly ambitious or profligate. This was reflected in the Shah's two surviving sons—Ismail, now imprisoned and Mohammad Khodabanda, always wasted.

The shah once confessed to Pari, "Do you know how much you remind me of my sister, the late Fulanesh Begum? She never minced words when it came to giving advice but always had my best interests at heart."

He recounted the incident when he wanted to poison Humayun because he was a staunch Sunni. Fulanesh, on learning about the same, had admonished her father, "You have enemies in all four directions: Ottomans, Uzbeks, Circassians and Franks! What will you achieve by assassinating Humayun and his sons, other than creating another enemy? Give him the freedom to leave and pursue his goals so that you have an ally on the eastern side."

"Pari, ever since then I have only trusted womenfolk for genuine advice. You too have wisdom and foresight like your *phuppo*. And you are my staunchest critic and ardent well-wisher!"

Pari knew she had to maintain a low profile and stay clear of controversies to emerge as the kingmaker once the shah died. Which also meant that she had to be careful no one saw her with Isa.

Pari continued socialising with her kith and kin until her father finished supper and retreated to his harem.

Pari quietly stepped out of the palace making sure no one saw her leave.

As she walked in the garden, Pari reflected, *I can't risk a scandal. There's too much at stake. It will undo all the progress I made so far. It has been so difficult to convince Abbu to let me have an office of my own at Kolah Farangi, away from the zenana.*

Kolah Farangi, situated at the southern corner of Chahar Bagh garden, was an elegant building with twenty slender wooden columns supporting the entrance pavilion which appeared as forty columns when reflected in the water. The first task that Pari performed on shifting to her new residence was the appointment of her servants, as she was aware that servants were the key perpetrators of palace gossip. Hence, she had appointed Ikram as her khansama. Ikram was a Black eunuch with a slit tongue, which meant he could neither suggest an illicit relation between them nor talk of her digressions.

She stopped abruptly and smiled when she spotted a food packet lying beside the fountain. Ikram had kept the food as instructed.

Pari quickly picked up the packet and walked towards the ruined fort at a hurried pace. Meimoon Ghal'eh lay at the south end of the town and Pari had ensured that the sentinel guarding the southern gate of the palace was one of her trusted guards. He ensured that the gate was left slightly ajar and kept a watch on the gate from behind the bushes while staying out of sight.

I hope I get to marry my handsome, brave, romantic Isa some day. Didn't the slave Iltutmish marry the ruler Qutb al-Din Aibak's daughter Qutub Begum?

Pari gingerly climbed up to the Parinama, her heart fluttering. Not a soul was present there. Then she spotted Isa. He was deep in slumber. *He looks so vulnerable and yet so desirable* Pari thought. *How do I wake him up?* Her eyes twinkled with irrepressible mischief as she released a drop of wine from the decanter on his lips. Isa woke up with a start.

It can't be raining at this time of the year, he wondered as he felt the moisture on his lips. As his eyes acclimatised to the surroundings, he saw Pari respledent in a green floral cloak, staring at him impishly. She looked radiant under the moonlight. Isa kept lying down admiring her glowing fair complexion, her sharp features, her thick black hair and her full red lips. Pari slowly brought her lips on Isa's and lightly kissed him.

"That's for being a good boy and waiting for me," said Pari.

The kiss ignited a strong desire in Isa's body, and he reached out to grab his Pari and draw her closer. Pari ached for his touch. It had been a while since they last met.

But she reprimanded him, "Isk, the night lies in wait for us. I am famished and I know you are too. Allah forbids us to make love when we are keeping rozah. So let us eat the food, drink the madeira and thank Allah that we are together. You can devour me later."

So, the two lovers sat next to each other on a boulder and gobbled down the naans and kebabs, while sipping the wine, when suddenly Isa looked northwards and exclaimed, "Why have people come out on the road with burning torches?"

They both looked towards Qazvin and could make out a few men running around with lanterns and torches. It appeared that the activities were happening inside Chahar Bagh. Pari panicked.

"Isk, I need to leave right now! Please destroy the food basket and return to your tent. Be careful my love."

Kissing Isa one last time, she sprinted towards the palace. As she made her way to Kolah Farangi, she wondered, *Are these people looking for me? They better not! I have to enter the garden premises without being spotted or else there could be trouble.*

Pari tried to breathe deeply to stay calm.

Fortunately, most inhabitants had retired to bed after the day-long fasting and the evening celebrations. Pari briskly made her way through the desolate surroundings and peeped through the Ali Qapu gate. She quickly slipped into the Chahar Bagh garden and moved behind the bushes, noticing that the nearest posse of searchers was still around one hundred metres away from her. She crouched, keeping behind the bushes, and approached Kolah Farangi. When she sensed she was close to the soldiers, she sat down on the ground, positioned as if she was resting, and shouted, "What's happening? Why are you all running about?"

The soldiers stopped in their tracks and looked at her in amazement. Wanting to not waste any more time, Pari sprung from behind the bush and approached them. She recognised that the soldiers were from Badi-al Zaman's troop.

"Begum, Prince Badi-al has been waiting for you at Kolah Farangi for a long time."

She knew she now had the narrative under control and confidently proceeded to her palace.

Prince Badi-al was anxiously waiting for Pari inside Kolah Farangi. He wanted to celebrate the Ashura with his family and had therefore travelled from Sistan to Qazvin to be with his ammi and begum. He had hoped to reach Qazvin before the Maghrib prayer, but got delayed, and it was almost midnight when he arrived at Kolah Farangi. He had hoped to surprise Pari, but she was nowehere to be seen, with her servants maintaining that the begum had not returned from the zenana, although Ikram appeared slightly flustered. Badi-al's mother, Zainab Sultan Khanum, the widow of his late father and now the consort of the shah, confirmed that Pari had left the palace over two hours back.

Pari, on seeing her mian, rushed towards him.

"Jaan, I am so happy to see you! I was feeling lonely and miserable without you and dreading returning to an empty bed. So, I was sitting in the garden, basking in the moonlight and fervently praying to Allah for you, and now you are here. *Allahu Akbar*!"

And as Pari retreated indoors with Badi-al, she thanked Allah again for the narrow escape.

Yet, someone had spotted Pari. On Isa's departure after the namaz, Ismail and his mates decided to have a quick meal and visit the red-light area which would be empty that night. But as they proceeded to a brothel, Ismail faintly identified Isa's silhouette disappearing towards Meimoon Ghal'eh. Ismail quickly excused himself, saying he would join his mates after he had checked on Isa. Ismail swiftly made his way towards Meimoon Ghal'eh. He decided not to climb up to the fort, but stay at its base, hidden behind a rock. There he fell asleep, until the sound of running footsteps woke him up, and he saw an alluring woman dart past him.

He followed her discreetly, till the palace gate. In the moonlight, he could see soldiers running helter-skelter with lanterns, when someone shouted out, "Let's go back to our camp. Princess Pari has been located."

Ismail was stunned. The missing pieces of the puzzle fell in place, and he understood why Isa was being so secretive. He was now excited and wanted to run back to his tent and quiz his brother on the romance, but as he turned, he saw four soldiers approaching him from the western side of the boundary wall. He wondered whether to confront them or run away. The soldiers must have read his mind for they shouted, "Hey, you *jasoos*, stand still!"

Ismail did not know that these were men from Badi-al's troop. As Ismail broke into a run, one of the soldiers shouted, "Catch him—he cannot escape. We must take the spy to Prince Badi-al!"

Ismail was sure he could outrun them, and once in Cepah Street, he could quickly disappear in one of the tents and the soldiers would not be able to find him. But as he gained speed, he spotted a few soldiers appearing on the eastern side. He realised he was cornered and he halted. He instantly drew out his sword, gripped the hilt with both his hands and decided to finally face his opponents.

Ismail had learnt all his sword manoeuvres from his brother and father while in Sarail. He rested his back against the wall. He opened his body, the left foot ahead of his right, and brought his sword forward. The soldiers running towards him too stopped in their tracks, and cautiously approached him with their drawn swords. Ismail observed the nine soldiers and realised he had to confront them individually, and the best way to do that was to go on the offensive while ensuring he stayed close to the wall so that no one could sneak up on him from behind.

The soldiers approached him deliberately for they realised he was a trained swordsman. Ismail wished Isa was alongside him to fight these soldiers, but he realised he must have retreated to his tent after the rendezvous with Pari. He smiled as he remembered his father's advice of attacking the side rather than the centre, "*Beta*, you never dive into the centre of the plate when you are served hot rice, but you nibble from the edge!"

Quickly, he shifted his stance to the left and attacked the corner soldier with such severity that he lost his arm and started screaming in agony. Ismail now shifted his stance to the right and as he did, he saw Isa running towards him. This must have distracted him as one soldier slashed at his left arm. The sharp pain made him flinch and he saw blood gushing out. Forgetting the basics of sword fighting, he darted at his closest rival, only to be again gashed from the side. Isa urgently wanted to join Ismail, but saw that the soldier's shrieks had attracted more troops and it would be foolhardy to join the fight. Instead, he shouted, "Ismail, why are you fighting with the shah's soldiers?"

The sword fight grinded to a halt.

Isa ran to embrace Ismail. Though the wounds were not deep, Ismail was bleeding profusely. As Isa wondered how to stop the bleeding, one of the soldiers asked, "If he is a soldier, why was he spying on the princess? And what were you doing watching from afar? Both of you must be secret agents of our enemies masquerading as soldiers. Come along, you have to meet the shah in the morning. Let us tie them up chaps."

Isa quickly opened his sarbandh and bandaged Ismail's wounds. As the brothers lay down tied together, Isa could sense that Ismail was losing consciousness due to loss of a lot of blood. As he fervently urged Ismail to stay awake and not close his eyes, Ismail looked at him and said, "Dada, I don't want to die!"

"Who's talking of dying?"

How will I show my face to Ammi if Ismail were to die! Allah, rescue us.

4

The Raj Badi of Sripur

CHAND ROY STEPPED OUT OF the temple sanctum, having just offered his prayers to Ma Tara. Tall, fair and well built, Chand did not look like a typical Bengali. Rather, he had a Caucasian look, with an oval face, a mop of red curly hair, thick black eyebrows, big black eyes, a prominent moustache which hid his small mouth and soft jaws. Chand's forefathers came down to Bengal from the North-Western Province almost two centuries ago. Standing on the porch, sporting a white dhoti, clean-shaven, bare chested, with a white shawl hanging next to his sacred thread, Chand surveyed Gangaridai, the fabled land that even Alexander loathed to conquer.

A staunch Shakta, Chand was always up before dawn to offer his prayers at the temple. He had installed their family deity—a two-foot blue idol of Goddess Tara—in an abandoned Buddhist monastery close to the Kali Ganga

River, when he was given the zamindari of the Bikrampur area by Emperor Humayun around seven years ago. He had strengthened the structure, constructed columns to support the dome and now the spectacular temple could be viewed miles away from the river. People marvelled at the eleven feet width of the temple walls and complimented him for constructing such a magnificent structure. Chand accepted all the adulation without divulging that he had only renovated the temple.

Around ninety feet south of the temple, Chand had constructed a two-storey mansion and named it Raj Badi after his forefather, Rajaram Deb, who had come down to Sonargaon on the instructions of the Delhi sultan, Muhammad Bin Tughlaq, to serve as the munshi of Governor Bahadur Khan and keep an eye on the accounts on behalf of the Delhi court. Chand had wanted the house to be closer to the temple, but his purohit had warned against that, saying it was not Vastu compliant.

Looking at the Raj Badi, Chand thought, *Success makes a man* and smiled. His forefathers, right from Rajaram, had been versatile in Farsi but Chand had also mastered Arabic. Fame of his proficiency in the languages reached Emperor Humayun who appointed Chand as a tehsildar in faraway Karnaata. And when Humayun returned as the emperor of India after defeating Sher Shah and saw that Chand had continued to serve his interests in Karnaata, he repaid Chand's dedication by awarding him the zamindari of Bikrampur. This was a hereditary title granted to Chand by the emperor, which meant his progeny would also enjoy the zamindari of the estate. This was the first instance in Bengal where a family inherited the zamindari rights, making him a landlord or *bhoumik*, as known in Bengali.

However, Emperor Humayun had a vested interest in granting land in Bikrampur. The Arakanese, whom the Bengalis referred to as Mogs, had captured the port town of Chittagong and its adjacent areas a year ago. The emperor was sure that the Burmese would now try to proceed westwards towards northern India, and he wanted a trusted lieutenant in that area.

Chand was thrilled to be honoured as the first bhoumik of Bengal, and that too of Bikrampur—the cradle of Bengal from time immemorial. Several rulers had their capital here in the past, including the Pala, Chandra and Sena dynastics. Bajrajogini village—which was the birthplace of the legendary Buddhist monk and scholar Atish Dipankar—was only six kilometres west, and next to it, in the village Rampal, Chand had seen the ruins of the Sena royal palace, Ballalbari.

Bikrampur, bordered by the mighty Padma to the west, the Dhaleshwari to the north, and the Meghna to the south and the east, was akin to an island, and Chand realised the island was easy to defend while providing escape routes for his army to retreat to the numerous islands of the Bengal Delta when overwhelmed. Chand had positioned cannons across the river frontiers, for the Afghans could attack from the west and north, while the Arakanese and Portuguese, whom the Bengalis called Harmads, could attack from the south and east.

However, it was a time of peace and prosperity for Chand and Bikrampur because north India was in turmoil. The

Afghans were busy fighting among themselves and the Mughals were trying to subjugate the Rajputs, allowing Chand to consolidate his control over vast stretches of eastern Bengal. He had also established trade relations with the Portuguese and assured them support in their confrontations with the Arakanese. He did turn a blind eye to their misdemeanours with the womenfolk on coastal Bengal, though he warned them against committing such crimes up the river.

The year 1563 was a lucky one for Chand. It brought into his life his daughter Sona. Today was her *annaprashan* ceremony. Chand was thrilled that his only child, after so many years of marriage, was a girl. He felt Goddess Lakshmi had entered his house. More importantly, the pandit on preparing her *thikuji* noted that Sona was destined to be a rani.

This was music to Chand's ears and just the right time for him to announce he was the first among the equals, and an opportune moment to repay those who sang disparagingly behind his back:

"*Chand Roy naam*
Zomidar oti adhya dosyu britti kam.
Tin laksha mudra khay kor nahi dey,
Nabab asoyan aile maariya bhagay.
Laskar banduk tope onek achhoy,
Nabab tahar songe juddhe na paroy.
Shakti mantre upasok durgotsab kori ...

(Chand Roy, leading zamindar and more, a bandit to the core! Spends to the max, yet does not pay tax, when the rulers come to ask, he takes them to task. Lascars he has in plenty—all armed with gun; seeing them—the soldiers run. A strong believer of Shakti, beheads tenants in the name of Bhakti—slaughter large number of goats and buffaloes; not even afraid of sacrificing cows and Brahmins!)"

As Chand started walking towards the Raj Badi, he looked towards the Meghna. The monsoon was over, but the water was yet to recede, and it appeared that Chand was standing on an island amidst an ocean. In the background, white *kash* flowers swayed in the breeze and fragrance of *shiuli* and jasmine filled the air. Tiny fishing boats, curved and narrow, were returning from the sea to deliver their first catch to the Raj Badi for the afternoon feast. Preparations had started in full swing under close supervision of his father Bhudeb Roy. Chand had made elaborate arrangements for entertaining the guests. Chand thought, *I want the guests to remember this celebration for years to come. Today is the day I am going to display my might and show my strength to the world.*

While his relatives had started arriving at Sripur almost a week back, Chand was keener on receiving and entertaining the leading doyens of Bengal. Invitation letters, with boxes of sweets and fruits, had been despatched to the dignitaries almost a month back. In another two hours' time, Padma and Meghna will be teeming with *goyna* boats, *bajras, malars* and *shuluks*. Chand hurried along. Normally, after finishing his puja, he would wait and admire the sunrise over the Meghna, and sunrises were beautiful especially during the month of Bhadro with the clear blue sky bordered in a myriad tinge of red.

Chand particularly wanted to spend time with Vikramaditya Sridhara Roy, the commander of Taj

Khan's army, and Raja Jagadananda Roy, the zamindar of Chandradwip. Like Chand, they were leading Kulin Kayasthas and Chand strongly believed that the unity of Bengal lay in the hands of the community.

Chand changed into a pristine white cotton dhoti and kurta, wore a thick gold chain with matching bracelets, applied oil on his hair and came down to the reception. His manager was already waiting there.

"How is it going, Sanatan?"

Sanatan pointed at the adjacent big drums, and replied, "Saheb, they are filled with *khejur ras, chitol muitha* is almost ready and as soon as the first guests arrive, the cooks will start frying *beguni, potol bhaja, chingri machh, rui machh* and *ilish machh. Shor bhaja, pitha* and sandesh have already been spread out."

Chand nodded and smiled.

"Let me know when any esteemed *atithi* arrives."

Chand picked up a *kansa* glass and poured himself some date juice, enjoying the thought that as the day progressed and the juice fermented, people would enthral in its potency. As he moved towards the portico, Chand noticed a distinguished-looking person had already arrived. He was tall, well built and looked slightly older than him.

Who is he? Chand thought to himself.

The gentleman smiled and said, "Namaskar. I am Ramdas, a Baiswara Rajput, son of Bhagirath Singh and grandson of Dhanapat Singh, the Kshatriya Raja of Oudh. My father was a diwan under Sultan Ghiyasuddin Mahmud Shah. Surely, you must have heard about my elder brother, Kalidas Gajdani."

"Yes, we know about Kalidas."

He paused and hesitantly asked, "But is it also not true that your brother fell in love with Ghiyasuddin's daughter, converted to Islam and married her?"

Ramdas sighed and replied, "Chand babu, you are an erudite person and I am sure you know how our faith and belief have been compromised because of these Muslim invaders. Remember what the Bhatta poets had to say—"*Ek ghar bhangiya tar holo saat bari; tin ghor barendro, tar dui ghor rarhi; dui ghor musalman, nosto anyojon, Basanta Rai'er bongsho banger bhuson* (One house broke to make way for three Barendras, two Rarhis, two Mussalmans and the last fell! Basanta Roy's progeny, Bengal's jewel!)!"

"Kalidas could not manage the diverse pulls of following the scriptures and serving a Muslim master, and I do not blame him. How do you expect Hindus to maintain their dharma in these trying times? The Brahmins are more worried about their personal benefits, and it is up to us Kayasthas to forget our differences, unite and support each other for Bengal's progress."

Chand was happy to learn that he was not the only one dreaming of a unified Bengal. *This is just the right opportunity to develop alliances with other interested parties and fight for a unified Bengal,* he reflected.

"So what happened to Gajdani's family?"

"You must be aware that Taj Khan killed Kalidas who had declared his independence in Sarail. My *bhaipos,* Isa and Ismail, were taken prisoners by him and sold as slaves. I have heard nothing about them since."

"You are in luck. Taj Khan's commander, Vikramaditya Sridhara Roy, will be joining us soon. Ask him to locate your nephews. Kayasthas and Kshatriyas need to stick to each other if we need our Bengal to survive."

And then he looked at the entrance and said, "Look who is here!"

"Sridhara babu, I must have done a lot of good work in my past life to be blessed with your visit."

Sridhara was wearing a white dhoti and kurta. He was of medium height, dark, slightly plump, with black hair, round face with black eyes and clean shaven but with a thick black moustache. Sridhara was a person who could be ignored but to one's peril. For behind the staid countenance lay a person who was exceedingly shrewd and brave, a person who had risen to the position of senapati in Taj Khan's army by always trusting his instincts and knowing which way the wind was blowing.

As Chand approached to embrace, Sridhara replied, "What are you saying? Please do not embarrass me! How could I turn down your invitation?"

What Chand had left unsaid was that Sridhara was blessed by a baby boy a year ago, and the astrologers had predicted that the offspring was going to commit patricide. Sridhara did not waste any time in getting the baby drowned at Gangasagar. Since then, he avoided invitations to annaprashan ceremonies. How tedious is a guilty conscience.

As Chand turned to introduce Ramdas to Sridhara, Sanatan announced, "The Chandradwip royal family is arriving!"

Chand immediately rushed out.

Chandradwip was the Dwarka of the east. Like Dwarka, the island used to routinely submerge and emerge from the ocean bed. As the wise men say, there are three constants in Chandradwip— rice, rivers and canals. But the foundation of the capital Kachua changed the social status of the Kayasthas in Bengal. Brahmins and Kayasthas from neighbouring Bikrampur flocked to Chandradwip.

As the saying goes "*Danujmardan raja chandradwip-pati, sei hoilo bangaja kayastha gosthipati* (Danujmardan—the king of Chandradwip—is the leader of Kayasthas in Bengal)." Paramananda Roy, a descendant of Danujmardan and the present king of Chandradwip, was the current Kayastha Kulapati of Bengal and Chand knew that if a Kayastha confederation was to be built, enlisting the support of Paramananda was critical.

As Chand hurried, he thought to himself, *I don't think Paramananda would be able to make it because of his old age, but I am sure he has sent his son Jagadananda. Would be nice to meet him again.*

But Raja Jagadananda Roy was nowhere to be seen. Instead, Chand spotted a young man. *Here, I have sent invitation to all Bengali nobles, as this is supposed to be a celebration of the Kulin Kayasthas. Yet, how dare the low-ranking Basus insult me by sending a young representative to this ceremomy. It is a slap on my face!*

The young scion touched his feet and said, "*Pronam.* I am Kandarpanarayan Roy, son of Jagadananda Roy. Baba sends his apologies and this letter."

As Chand opened the letter, Kandarpanarayan said, "Baba has been warned by his *jyotish* that he will die from drowning, and hence he now refuses to travel over water."

Seeing Chand's crestfallen face, Kandarpanarayan smiled.

"Knowing how important this occasion is for you, my *dadu* has come to visit you. But he finds it difficult to walk and has therefore requested whether you can join him with your esteemed guests on his *bajra*."

A delighted Chand warmly embraced Kandarpanarayan, and said, "That would be my honour. Now, why don't you go upstairs to the *andar mahal*."

He turned around and called out, "Sanatan! Sanatan! Come quickly! Take Kandarpanarayan to Kedar babu and send the other important guests to the bajra."

Chand walked swiftly towards the ghat.

5

Qaidi Isa Khan

INCARCERATED IN A CELL IN a castle, Isa was downcast. It had been over four months since that eventful day in August when Isa and Ismail were captured. He had been taken prisoner and brought to court the next day. As Isa had entered Shah Tahmasp's court, he recalled the excitement of his first visit. He sighed and muttered to himself, "How the times have changed." On entering the court, Isa immediately spotted Pari sitting behind the shah but enraptured in discussions with a person whom he did not recognise. *Is that her mian*? He thought. Pari never even bothered to look up and glance at him.

Are we strangers already?

The case proceeding was bizarre, to say the least. It was argued that Ismail was caught spying and had died due to injuries suffered while attacking the soldiers. Isa wondered, *What was Ismail doing peeping though the Ali Qapu gate so late at night*?

The official asked, "What were you doing at the scene?

Isa dispassionately stated, "I was indisposed on the Ashura night, and had retired early to my tent but around midnight, when I had gone to check on Ismail, I found his tent empty. I then wandered into the town to locate him. After a while, I saw him in a scuffle with the Safavid soldiers. I had to rush in when my beloved brother fell down."

The shah nodded. His spies had corroborated Isa's story. The shah recognised the need to identify rebels and traitors early and imprison them, and that is what had compelled him to keep his son in confinement.

Looking at the rubies on his hand, the emperor reflected how the stone was considered to be the manifestation of the spilt blood of a murdered and unavenged king.

He pondered, *What to do with Isa? If I grant amnesty to him, he could plot my assassination to extract revenge for his brother's death. After all, blood is thicker than water...*

The shah finally announced, "Isa to be locked up until further instructions."

It was important to keep his friends close, and his enemies closer.

I will never escape from this highly guarded prison. How will I climb down a mountain on foot? Moreover, what's the point? The terrain all around for miles is rocky and barren.

Isa was resigned to his fate. His days now consisted of waking up before dawn, performing morning ablutions, participating in the Fajr prayer with other inmates, having breakfast and then retreating to his cell. They again congregated around noon for the Zuhr prayer and lunch and reassembled at dusk for the Maghrib prayer and supper.

The only way he managed to deal with the reality was by escaping into the past.

Lying in his cold, dark cell, staring at the stone walls, all alone, Isa contemplated, *Who would believe I was once the heir to the Bengal throne? Or that I originally hail from an orthodox Hindu family and that my great grandfather ruled Oudh. Love, success and happiness are so fleeting, and everything is so fragile and finite.*

While his father loved Isa deeply, he never discussed his past.

"Your abba had lost a discourse to your *mausa* Danishmand and had therefore embraced Islam," his ammi had once said. Isa seriously doubted the veracity of the story. *If my uncle Danishmand was such an excellent debater, lots of Hindu scholars would have converted to Muslim. Yet, I don't know of anyone who did.*

Early on in life, Isa realised there were several versions of the past and it was always the conqueror whose story dominated. As a young child, Isa had heard rumours that Sultan Ghiyasuddin was an incompetent, pleasure-seeking ruler, but never dared to ask his ammi who never spoke ill of her father.

Isa knew that the period of reign by Hussain Shah followed by his son Nasiruddin Nusrat Shah was regarded as the golden age of Bengal. The Bangla language flourished under the royal patronage. This was a period of peace and prosperity because of the sultan's liberal attitude towards his Hindu subjects. This was the time when the Bhakti cult was spreading throughout Bengal due to Chaitanya Mahaprabhu.

But Isa would often wonder, *Was the era really the golden age*? Hussain Shah executed over 12,000 soldiers when he ascended the throne. Poets' lauded the execution as punishment for vandalising Gaur. But Isa often wondered whether it was directed towards eliminating rebels and future threats.

Ghiyasuddin had created enemies among the high court officials on usurping the throne after murdering his nephew, and therefore, Isa's paternal grandfather from distant Oudh was appointed as the dewan because the sultan wanted trusted, non-partisan advisers.

Isa's father would often rue, "The new advisers were not acquainted with the complexities of Bengal and the kind of political equations that needed to be set. This led to a lot of challenges and setbacks."

In fact, one night when Syeda was not around, Sulaiman had lamented, "We would have still ruled over Bengal if Sultan Ghiyasuddin and his advisers had the foresightedness of his predecessors. See how the sultan's elder brother Nusrat had married Delhi sultan Ibrahim Lodi's daughter so that the marauding Lodi chief, who was plundering north India, did not advance towards Bengal. This allowed Nusrat to consolidate his rule in Bengal."

Isa had often heard from his ammi that his abbu had hastily fled the royal palace one night. It perturbed him how such a strong kingdom could crumble overnight.

Sulaiman continued, "War should not be fought on ego but based on strategy and assessment of one's own strength.

When Babar captured Delhi, the Afghan lords of north India mostly moved towards the east and declared themselves as chieftains. Most dynasties in the past ruled Bengal from the Bikrampur–Sonargaon area as the complicated riverine topography of that area offered a natural barrier from enemies. A retreat by Sultan Ghiyasuddin towards south-east Bengal was required, especially since warfare had been redefined."

"How so Abbu?"

"Babar, with a small army of around fifteen thousand soldiers routed the estimated one lakh soldiers of Ibrahim Lodi's army at the First Battle of Panipat in 1526 through use of cannons, and new war tactics like *tulughma* and *araba*."

"What are tulughma and araba, Abbu?

"Tulughma is a military tactic or formation which meant dividing the whole army into various units like left, right and centre, which enabled a small army to quickly surround the enemy from all sides, with the centre forward division having arabas or bullock carts placed in front, which protected the cannons. In that sense, the araba is a mobile artillery weapon. The bullock carts were held together by ropes and the cannons fired from behind them. The sound of the cannons frightened Lodi's elephants, causing them to trample Lodi's own men, while Babar's men on horses quickly encircled them.

"If the war had continued for another hour, Babar's army would have been decimated as they were extremely tired. Beta, understand the importance of perseverance and that the battle is never lost until the last shot is fired."

Isa reflected, *History is all about infighting, deceit, betrayal and survival of the fittest. A community prospered when peace and stability prevailed. A good ruler should be liberal, strong, wise, aware of one's strengths and weaknesses and adept at building relationships.*

"Sultan Ghiyasuddin should not have confronted Sher Shah. Nusrat Shah had allowed the Lohanis to prosper in Bihar as they acted as a buffer against the Mughal onslaught."

"The Battle of Surajgarh almost thirty years ago seriously dented Bengal's military pride and prompted Sher Shah to proceed towards Bengal to capture Sultan Ghiyasuddin. Your ammi and I could barely manage to escape Gaur as Sher Shah plundered and burnt the city."

Isa pondered as he continued to look at the damp ceiling, *Strategy is so vital to protect one's sovereignty. I wonder how Bengal has progressed in these interim years. How I wish I could see Ammi again and breathe the air of my land ...*

Unknown to Isa, Bengal was in a crisis. Following Islam Shah's death in 1553, a factional tussle erupted in the Suri dynasty. Islam's son was killed by his maternal uncle Mubariz who ascended the throne with the title of Adil Shah, but was eventually defeated and killed by the new sultan Ghiyasuddin Bahadur Shah II.

Ghiyasuddin II ruled for around half a decade, after which his brother took charge, but the new sultan was assassinated within two years, and his son also met the same fate within a few months. Shortly afterwards, the Karrani dynasty took control of Bengal. Taj Khan Karrani, erstwhile governor of Oudh—which was once ruled by Isa Khan's ancestors—

was now the sultan of Bengal. The same Taj Khan who had assassinated Isa's father.

Taj Khan had repressed Bengal for the past three decades and realised that history was a repetitive story of sons and fathers murdering each other, relatives and in-laws feuding, and trusted advisers becoming betrayers. He therefore welcomed Bengali Hindus to high position in his army and administration, for he felt that they were too timid to revolt. Hence, he had promoted Sridhara as his army senapati. And when Sridhara recommended Ramdas's name as his wazir, he quickly accepted. Little could he realise how his decisions would change the political history of Bengal!

6

Will Syeda's Prayers Be Answered?

AD 1564

IT WAS SPRING—THE TIME for harvest collection. Ramdas as Taj Khan's wazir, arrived in Sonargaon, ostentatiously to collect taxes, but actually to trace Syeda and Fatima. Ramdas was childless, hence he wanted a progeny to carry on the family genes. Social barriers were crumbling among the elite—even Emperor Akbar's favourite consort was a Hindu—and Ramdas had therefore reconciled to his brother's interfaith marriage. He had been able to trace the journey of Isa and came to know, with help from Sridhara, that his nephew was imprisoned in distant Qazvin. He was unaware of the crime committed by Isa but was told that he had been charged for spying on the Safavid kingdom. It broke his heart to learn about Ismail's murder.

Since religious sway held more clout than political compulsions for the Shah Tahmasp, Ramdas decided to enlist the support of Danishmand to influence the Shah. After all, Sayyid Ibrahim Danishmand was a descendant of the Sufi priest, Sayyid Nasiruddin, who claimed descendancy from Hazrat Ali, regarded as the rightful successor to Prophet Muhammad by Shia Muslims.

His quest led him to Sarail.

Ramdas was shocked on arriving at Sarail. It resembled a jungle and showed no signs of habitation. But he witnessed a panorama of flame and colour as *shimul, palash, krishnachura* and *radhachura* were in full bloom. Ramdas was wondering what to do when he heard the faint melody of a flute. He followed the sound and came across a lad sitting on the branch of a mango tree, playing a flute. The tune reminded Ramdas of the song "*O Behula ami moile amay niye bhasaiyo bhela* (Behula, when I die, float me in a raft)."

Ramdas barked at the boy, "What are you doing sitting on a tree? Where is everyone?"

The boy, thin, dark and hardly ten years old was startled. He jumped down from the tree, tightened his dhoti and asked, "Who are you?"

"I am the Bengal king's messenger! I want to meet your baba–ma."

Reluctantly, the lad led Ramdas inside the forest.

As they went deep inside the forest, Ramdas feared that a tiger might attack, but the boy seemed sure of his way.

"How much further? Hope you are not taking me for a ride!" But the boy ran into a clearing and disappeared. Ramdas saw that they had now come across an open space in the forest and a few mud houses lay scattered. He was sure that the lad was hiding in one of the houses, and as he approached the nearest house, a middle-aged woman, wearing a green sari, ran out of the hut holding a vegetable cutter.

She screamed, "One more step and I will cut my neck with this *boti*!"

Ramdas begged her, "Ma, please do not do anything like that!"

Seeing his worried expression, the woman relaxed.

She loudly whistled and some menfolk arrived almost out of thin air.

Ramdas decided to exchange some pleasanatries to lighten the charged atmosphere.

"Why do you people live so deep in the jungle?"

A young man replied, "Saheb, the Mogs and the Harmads have been regularly invading the Mymensingh and Comilla areas and we have no choice but to move westwards towards Sonargaon and Bikrampur. Now these Mogs are building a temple to commemorate their conquest of Bengal and they require labourers. Hence, they are frequently raiding the hinterland to enlist us as slaves. Further, the Harmads are raiding and looting the countryside!"

Ramdas nodded his head. Chand Roy's presence in Sripur meant that these goons were no longer sailing upstream.

"You villagers have done the right thing by moving inside the forest. I need your help with one thing. Can you direct me to Sulaiman's *mahal*? Does his family still reside there?"

An old man shook his head and quietly said, "Saheb, when Sulaiman was beheaded and his sons enslaved, their wives moved to Sonargaon. The palace is in ruins, engulfed by the forest, and no one stays there."

"*Dhanyavad.*"

Taking their leave, Ramdas travelled towards the Shitalakshya River and then moved downstream towards Sonargaon.

Sonargaon was the headquarters of Bengal under the eighteenth Sultan of Delhi Muhammad Bin Tughlaq. Just like Sripur, it was a well-protected island, bounded on the east by the Meghna, on the south by the Dhaleshwari, on the west by the Shitalakshya and on the north by the Meghna. Sonargaon became a short-lived independent state in the mid-fourteenth century under Fakhruddin Mubarak Shah, and Ibn Batuta who sailed through the port of Sonargaon during that time described Fakhruddin as "a distinguished sovereign who loved strangers, particularly the fakirs and sufis".

Not surprisingly, Sonargaon soon developed into a major centre of Sufism. The later rulers of the Bengal Sultanate ensured that Sonargaon was a fortified river port which could be used as a base for attacking neighbouring kingdoms like Tipperah, Mrauk U and Kamata.

On landing at Sonargaon and enquiring about Danishmand, the country folks immediately directed Ramdas towards his *khanqah* opposite the Goaldi Mosque. The name Goaldi Mosque was familiar to Ramdas. It had been constructed during the reign of Sultan Alauddin Hussain Shah. Sultan Ghiyasuddin gave the governorship of Sonargaon to his son-in-law Sayyid Ibrahim Danishmand, who had settled there around three decades ago. Sonargaon was already a developed centre of Muslim learning and Persian literature. It had a well-reputed madrasa, attracting students from all across the subcontinent. Danishmand was now maintaining these institutions.

It was late morning and Ramdas wanted to catch Danishmand before he retired for namaz, lunch and siesta.

As Ramdas made his way through the town, he observed its prosperity and reflected on the importance of a strong military administration for peace and prosperity. Gaur and Sonargaon were the two most important cities of Bengal, with Gaur prevailing in land campaigns during the dry seasons of winters and summers, while Sonargaon provided the naval base for monsoon challenges.

Further, Sonargaon generated significant revenues for the Bengal Sultanate due to its muslin, calico and rice production; and being a key financier for the Bengal Sultanate, a royal court and a mint had been established in this port town. Sonargaon had to be protected at all costs and even Sher Shah Suri had understood its importance, ensuring that the Grand Trunk Road that linked Bengal to Central Asia originated here.

Ramdas marvelled at the remarkable architecture and intricate facades of the buildings all around. The Persian influence was heavy but that was not a surprise as Persians and Turks had been settling down in Sonargaon for the past three centuries. As soon as Ramdas spotted the Goaldi Mosque, he halted and stood admiring the single-dome square mosque, built of red bricks, with four corner towers. The walls had elaborate artwork.

Suddenly, Ramdas noticed a burqa-clad lady approaching him.

The moment Syeda Momena Khatu caught sight of Ramdas, she walked towards him with hesitant steps. She was now a pale shadow of the beautiful damsel she once was. She would often think about the past and blame herself. *If only I hadn't fed beef to Sulaiman. Kismet is not kind to me because of my misdeeds. Hai Allah, forgive me for my sins and bring me back my sons.* Danishmand would often comfort her by saying, "*Allah hi jaane kaun bashr hai* (God alone knows the true nature of people)!"

Syeda now devoted her life to Allah and numbed her memories to deal with the tremendous loss and unbearable pain. Memories flooded her mind when she spotted Ramdas.

He looks so much like Sulaiman ... just older. What is he doing here? I don't think I have any strength in me to bear any bad news. Apprehending the worst, she screamed, "Hai Allah!"

And then her mind went blank and she fainted.

Fatima was watching her mother-in-law from inside the mosque. Her curiousity was heightened on seeing her hesitantly approach a tall, elderly, moustached stranger who looked regal, and then collapsing on the ground. Alarmed, she tugged her ammi and pointed outside. Fatima was startled when her ammi gasped and whispered, "Sulaiman!"

Fatima was very young when her father-in-law was beheaded and had no clear memory of him. But on hearing his name, she incredulously asked, "Ammi, how can *sasurji* be alive?"

Their conversation attracted the attention of Danishmand who immediately rushed out of the mosque. Fatima and her ammi followed him. He was horrified to see Syeda lying unconscious next to a stranger. He quickly instructed his wife and daughter to tend to her.

Glaring at the stranger, he asked, "Who are you?"

"I am Ramdas, brother of Kalidas, and I am here to meet Danishmand."

Danishmand nodded and said, "Follow me."

Danishmand was now nearing sixty. Dressed in a white *khirqah* and a pointed white headdress, it was his white flowing beard that attracted attention. He was now the most venerated Sufi scholar in the subcontinent and is believed to be one of the first to preach and operate in Bengal for the Qadiriyya Sufi order, which was founded in Baghdad in the twelfth century.

They sat on the outdoor lounge. Hope flickered for his daughter when Danishmand heard the purpose of Ramdas's visit. He said, "You are correct in your understanding that we trace a direct chain back to Prophet Muhammad. But as you know we are Sunnis, and Shah Tahmasp is a Shia ..."

"Danish Bhai, surely, there must be Sufi saints you know who trace their chain through Ali ibn Abi Talib, the Prophet's son-in-law whom the Shias consider to be his rightful successor!"

Danishmand smiled.

"It is strange that you should mention this. We, of the Qadiriyya order, trace our lineage to Prophet Muhammad through Ali."

"Danishmand means wise and not without reasons are you called Malik al-Ulama (King of Scholars). If you write an official letter with your lineage, Shah Tahmasp will not be able to distinguish whether you are a Sunni or a Shia. I would implore you to write a *khat* to him. I will get it delivered."

Danishmand chuckled.

"You are being too kind Ramdasji. However, I am better known here as Qutb-ul-Ashiqeen—the Saint of Lovers for my deep love for the Divine. Of course, I will do anything to bring love back to Fatima's life. *Bismillah Allah hu Akbar*!"

By this time, Syeda regained consciousness. She instantly remembered why she had fainted and asked her elder sister and daughter-in-law, "Where is Ramdas?"

Before they could reply, Syeda saw her *humzulf* and *dewar* walking towards them. Embarrassed, she got up quickly to greet them and realised that her niqab had fallen. She cursed herself and swiftly bent down to pick it up. And as she adjusted her niqab and turned to face them, she wondered, *Why is Danishmand smiling*?

Danishmand addressed Fatima, "Beti, this is your husband's *chacha*. He brings news that your *shohar* is well and we are now going to arrange for his return to Sonargaon."

Fatima erupted in joy.

Syeda smiled, said a silent prayer to Allah and quietly asked, "What about Ismail?"

Unfortunately, she got no answer.

Hai Allah, not he too.

"Danishmand, I need to leave now for a quick lunch. I shall return in the late afternoon to collect the letter."

Danishmand slowly nodded and grimly said, "Unfortunately, because of our different religions, I could not even offer you a glass of water. For the same reason,

I cannot request you to stay for lunch. See you later. *Khuda Hafiz.*"

Ramdas retired to his bajra and enjoyed a leisurely lunch of rice, dal, vegetables, fish curry and fruits, before leaving for Danishmand's khanqah. On arrival, he was immediately taken into the *sahn*. There in the open courtyard, he saw Danishmand writing a letter in Persian. Like most educated and high-ranking Hindus, Ramdas had been taught Farsi and Arabic from a young age—a practice that had started among the Hindu elite in the early thirteenth century to ensure court favour.

He read the letter:

> Shahnama-yi Shahi Shah Tahmasp—Adab. I am Malik al-Ulama Sayyid Ibrahim Danishmand, son of Sayyid Musafir son of Sayyid Sirajuddin son of Sayyid Nasiruddin Ispahsalar son of Hasan Arabi son of Khwaja Daud son of Khwaja Abul Fazl son of Khwaja Abul Farah son of Muhammad al-Mahdi son of Hasan al-Askari son of Ali an-Naqi son of Muhammad al-Taqi son of Ali al-Ridha son of Musa al-Kadhim son of Ja'far al-Sadiq son of Muhammad al-Baqir son of Zayn al-Abidin son of Hazrat Husayn son of Hazrat Ali. I am a direct descendant from the Prophet's son-in-law Ali ibn Abi Talib. I gather from my good sources that my son-in-law Isa Khan is imprisoned in your empire. I entreat you to release him and Allah's blessings will be on you.

Ramdas was incredulous. Surely, Danishmand had got his ancestors wrong for there were only eighteen links from Danishmand to Ali. The Prophet was born in the sixth century AD and it was improbable that only eighteen direct descendants linked Danishmand to the Prophet over a period of one thousand years, which meant that the gap between each generation was on an average fifty-five years. But Ramdas reflected that the letter was a compelling document and truth should never get in the way of a good story. He therefore waited for Danishmand to finish and seal the letter.

Danishmand finally said, "It is a few months for the Hajj. It has been my lifelong desire to perform the Hajj. Let me also travel with you and personally entreat the shah for Isa's *rihai*!"

7

The Rihai

AD 1564

IT WAS MID-MORNING. ISA LOOKED up at the small window near the eastern side of the rooftop and tried to see whether he could spot any birds. The sun's glare caught him in the eyes, and he turned back. On the western wall, he had made it a practice of etching a stone mark at the beginning of a day, crossing them at the end of every seventh day, to maintain a weekly count of his prison stay. Now, as he turned and looked at the illuminated stone etchings, he counted the marks and realised he had spent forty-nine weeks in the castle. He noticed he had marked the end of Ramadan over eleven weeks back.

He thought, *Another Islamic year is coming to an end and the holy month of Muharram will start soon tomorrow. Will I ever get to meet Pari again? Does she even care any more ? Do I have to spend a lifetime in this cold cell?*

Suddenly he heard the wooden pill lock of his cell being opened. *What an unusual time for the guards to visit me.*

The guards escorted Isa to the warden's room where he saw a few Safavid soldiers also present.

Ahmed remarked, "The shah says that you are no longer a prisoner and has ordered that you be presented at his court."

Isa let out a sigh of relief.

"Why is the shah pardoning me?"

He got a blank look in response from the warden.

"Your clothes and belongings are kept in your cell. Feel free to change. We leave tomorrow".

Isa returned to his cell and found his belongings had been kept in one corner of the room. The green salwar and jameh were laid out on his bed. As he picked the garments, he noticed the bloodstains of Ismail. *I can never again wear this outfit.*

Isa changed into a blue salwar and a white jameh, the same one that he had worn to the shah's court the first time. His experiences had made him superstitious, and he now believed in luck and providence. As he picked up a pair of his *nagra* and slipped them on, he felt elated as being a barefoot prisoner was humiliating.

Since Isa was no longer a prisoner, he now stepped out of the cell and walked around freely in the castle, even going up to the tower to survey the surroundings. He thought, *What a lovely view! This castle is virtually impregnable, with deep valleys surrounding the fortress and making it impossible to access from the eastern and western sides. I wonder who built this castle. Let me ask the warden.*

"I am not sure who constructed the fort but I know it was built during the Hashshashin period. Why don't you join me for namaz and lunch for more chit-chat?

Isa gladly accepted.

So, as they enjoyed the lunch, Isa commented in Farsi what a welcoming change it was to devour soft, fluffy breads after months of surviving on stale food. *Niagran* Ahmed, who was usually very stern and authoritarian with the inmates and had hardly ever spoken to Isa except for growling on a couple of occasions to speed up their chores, was now relaxed and asked, "What food from home do you miss the most?"

Isa thought for a while and said, "Mango!"

"What kind of food is that?"

Isa winked at Ahmed and replied, "You have not tasted mangoes! Amir Khusrau had this to say of the mango—"*Aam Naghza Tarin Mewa Hindustan* (Mango is the fairest fruit of India)."

Ahmed was astonished.

"Mango cannot be better than our watermelon. I always thought you were a Persian. You look so much like us, but you are a Hindustani! Do people in Hindustan also speak Farsi?"

"I am a Bengali from a region further east of Hindustan called Bengal. It is more than four thousand kilometres from here and there we speak Bengali!"

"*Tauba tauba*!"

Isa smiled.

"But nothing can beat the sweetness of the watermelon here."

The lunch and Isa's humility must have endeared Ahmed for while Isa was having his afternoon siesta, he was woken up by Ahmed who had brought the prison barber along.

"*Naai,*" he said, "please give my friend a good haircut and trim", and then he quipped, "You looked so elegant when you first came here that I mistook you for royalty and thought the shah had sentenced another one of his sons or sons-in-law to prison, until I was told that you had been imprisoned for being an accomplice of spying on the palace. Since you are going back to the king's court, you must appear elegant. You look like a faqir now."

Isa looked at the barber's mirror.

Indeed, I am looking like a mendicant in this flowing hair and long beard.

Isa went to bid farewell to his fellow inmates at dusk, but found everyone was avoiding him. *Maybe they are not acknowledging my presence because I look so different now after shaving and not wearing prison clothes.*

As Isa retired to his cell for the last night, he wondered, *Did Pari have a role to play in my rihai? How could she persuade the shah? I hope the emperor is not planning to execute me.* The precariousness of his position prevented him from falling asleep.

The next day, Isa started on his journey to Qazvin with the soldiers at daybreak. He felt good sitting on a horse, and as they raced downhill over the rocky terrain, Isa marvelled at the castle's construction and how it allowed the tower watchers an unobstructed view for miles. Soon, the castle was a speck in the background, and they galloped through the sparse vegetation of the countryside. It was midday when they arrived in Qazvin.

Isa's inquisitiveness made him straightaway proceed to the shah's court, and as he entered, he noticed the emperor was yet to arrive. The court was relatively empty, and while some members of the Kizilbash were there, what caught his attention were a group of soldiers who appeared to be from Bengal and who were dressed in green uniforms. *They look like soldiers from Taj Khan Karrani's army. But why are they here? Has there been a rebellion in Bengal and people want the old dynasty back? Or do the Karranis want to eliminate all challengers with linkages to the throne? I am not liking this at all!*

Danishmand called out, "Isa, come sit next to me."

Isa was amazed at seeing Danishmand. He looked significantly older than when he had last met him. His skin was wrinkled, facial hair had covered his face, but his green eyes looked the same.

"How nice to finally meet someone from my family. How are Fatima and Ammi?"

"They are all fine and eagerly waiting for your return!"

This was music to Isa's ears. "What are those *sipahis* from Taj Khan's army doing here?"

Before Danishmand could answer, Shah Tahmasp walked into the court. An entourage of loyal courtiers followed. As everyone in the court arose and bowed, the royal herald announced, "Sayyid Ibrahim Danishmand *haazir ho* (Sayyid Ibrahim Danishmand, present yourself)."

Danishmand arose, genuflected and said, "Shahnama-yi Shahi Shah, I am Sayyid Ibrahim Danishmand, son of Sayyid Musafir, son of ..."

But the shah interrupted Danishmand, "Qutb-ul-Ashiqeen, your reputation precedes you. You need no introduction. It is my privilege and my honour to receive you. I know you are a direct descendant of our Ali. My father, Shah Ismail I, when he founded the Safavid Empire, invited Sayyids from the Arabic world to come and settle here. I don't know why he missed out on Hindustan. But I am really indebted to your brethren from Arabia for spreading Twelver Shiism throughout our region.

"Ever since your messengers arrived with your letter, I have been eagerly awaiting your arrival. I also arranged for Isa to be here. He is free to go back with you. However, please join me at my palace for dinner."

Danishman agreed.

"It would be my pleasure, Shahenshah!"

At dusk, after offering namaz at the Jameh mosque, Danishmand and Isa walked towards the grand Ali Qapu Palace. As they waited in the hall, Isa was fascinated by the brilliantly painted interiors, which featured a multitude of paintings, including several scenes of battles and audiences held by the shah.

One particular fresco caught the attention of the visitors Shah Tahmasp, dressed in a yellow sherwani, entertaining a distinguished-looking guest dressed in yellow kurta, while three nautch girls danced, and their entourage watched. As they both admired the painting, the shah walked up behind them, along with his bodyguard—an impressive, towering black personality.

"Salam, meet my personal guard Masood. I see you both are connoisseurs of art too. You must come upstairs and see my Shahnameh collection."

As they proceeded upstairs, Isa enquired, "Shah Tahmasp, I am very curious about the person sitting with you in that painting hung in the hall downstairs."

"I am surprised you do not recognise your badshah, Humayun! This was taken during the Novrouz festival."

Danishmand said, "Humayun has never been our badshah. After Ghiyasuddin, I consider only Allah as my badshah!"

Unlike the ground floor, the hall on the first floor had open balconies at the four corners with the cool, fresh breeze blowing in.

"This is the music and entertainment room, but I mostly come here to admire the paintings."

As Danishmand and Isa looked closer, they saw what appeared as coloured tiles were actually paintings measuring probably one square foot. And there were hundreds of them.

"These are the illustrated manuscripts of the Shahnameh, our national epic. If you study these manuscripts closely, you will notice the hand paintings have couplets calligraphed alongside."

Danishmand congratulated the shah for such an epic collection.

"The world will ever be grateful to you for being such a committed patron of the art. But what prompted you to initiate such a massive project?"

"Actually, the credit goes to my father who commissioned these paintings to assert his legitimacy as a strong and stable ruler among his subjects. I have just continued with his legacy."

"Shah Tahmasp, could you please arrange a tour of the Shahnameh manuscript sequentially?"

"Most certainly! Masood, call Dost Muhammad."

Over the next forty-five minutes, the royal artist Dost Muhammad regaled the three with tales from the court of Guyumars and exploits of Rostam.

Danishmand was mesmerised.

"The paintings are exquisite, but the calligraphy is even better. Shahnama-yi Shahi, the world must know this history."

"I am thinking of gifting the collection to the Ottomans."

"That is an excellent idea ..."

Someone coughed behind them.

All of them turned. There was a person wearing a niqab standing at the top of the staircase and Isa recognised Pari's bewitching eyes. The shah turned to his guests and said, "Sayyid Ibrahim Danishmand and Isa Khan, may I have the pleasure of introducing you to my *beti* Pari Khan Khanum."

Turning to his daughter, he asked, "Yes, Pari?"

"Abbu Jaan, the *khana* has been served upstairs and is turning cold."

"Danishmand, we will go through the remaining manuscripts tomorrow."

"Huzoor, we are starting for Bengal tomorrow. My wife, sister-in-law and daughter are all eagerly awaiting our return and I want to be back at the earliest."

The shah pondered for a moment and then replied, "I fully understand your wishes. You will be my *mehman* tonight and we will complete the journey of the

Shahnameh later after our dinner. I hope that is fine with you too, Isa."

"Shahnama-yi Shahi, since I am returning tomorrow, I want to go and meet my old mates at Cepah Street after dinner. Danishmand can stay here at the palace and I will be back here, latest by dawn."

The shah nodded.

"Let's proceed for dinner without wasting any more time."

8

A Night to Remember

AD 1564

STARING AT THE CRESCENT MOON, Pari pondered about her life, *Here I am a married lady awaiting the arrival of a married man to enjoy a few fleeting moments of intimacy before fate prevails.*

Sitting on a bench outside the Kolah Farangi, hidden behind the bushes, the princess eagerly awaited the arrival of Isa. Dinner had been a sombre affair, with the emperor engaged in conversation with Danishmand while Isa feasted on the traditional lavish spread laid out before him. The appetisers included *ash-e doogh, imam bayildi* and *ash-e mash piazou*; the main course had *doimaj, shirin polo, bademjan polo, kuku shirin* and *gheimeh nesar*, apart from various types of naans, kebabs, baklavas and fruits, including melons, citrus fruits, Chinese gooseberries, dates, cherries, pomegranates, peaches, raisins, grapes, watermelons, walnuts, almonds and pistachios.

Pari and her sister-in-law, Khayr al-Nisa Begum were the only two women present at the dinner. Though Pari suspected Khayr was present more to keep an eye on her husband, Mohammad Khodabanda. Pari always maintained a distance from the unscrupulous Khayr, and thus partook her food in silence, while listening to the animated discussions between her father and Danishmand.

As Pari waited in the garden, she couldn't help but think, *I wish Isq had told me he was married himself instead of hearing it from his father-in-law. Though it is so good to know he is also a Sayyid. Sayyids marry only in their community ...*

She smiled as her hopes soared. Pari now felt herself fortunate to be his paramour. Isa's new cloak of respectability made Pari's admiration for him soar.

When Pari heard that Isa had been pardoned, she could sense that it was a matter of a few days after which Isa would return to Bengal. *I want to make these last few days memorable for both of us.* After the court was adjourned, Pari rushed to Kolah Farangi.

"*Ikram! Ikram! Jaldi aao.*"

Ikram came running.

"*Ji,* Begum. *Kya hukum?*" he asked bowing.

"Ikram call an *araish gar,* I want to pamper myself!"

A beautician was summoned. She applied black mud pack on Pari's face, trimmed her nails and waxed her. She always dreaded waxing sessions and avoided them like plague, but she was hirsute.

Isa has always complimented my soft baby skin and I am in no mood to disappoint him tonight, Pari thought, as she took a deep breath when the beautician applied hot wax on her arm.

After the excruciating depilation experience, Pari bathed herself in rose water and changed into a zardozi chemise. She lavishly spread attar on herself, draped herself in a flaming red velvet robe accentuated with wide, gold-embellished sashes, put on a white chahar-qad on the crown of her head accompanied with a chin strap adorned with pearls, and rushed to attend her father's dinner.

Where is Isa?

Pari was disappointed to see officials and family members in the dinner hall. There was no sign of her father or her Isa. She ran down in search of the shah and smiled to herself when she spotted him with the guests admiring the Shahnameh manuscripts. She overheard Danishmand state that they would be returning to their homeland the following day. She knew she had to act quickly. *I hope I get to meet him alone tonight. Time is running out.* Knowing that this was probably the best spot to approach Isa, she fell behind her father and Danishmand and whispered into Isa's ears, "Meet me near the bench in the bagh after the dinner."

Given the narrow corridor of time, she had returned to Kolah Farangi after Isa had taken the Shah's leave, gone upstairs to inform her servants she was retiring, removed her *ghunghroos* and then descended from the backstairs to the garden. As Pari reflected on her love and life, she spotted Isa slowly walking down the boulevard.

As Isa approached Pari, he thought about his strange predicament. *After living a life as a slave for over a decade,*

I will finally be free. I can't wait to be among my people and savour Amma's home-cooked food. But I can't leave Qazvin immediately. I want to spend some time with Pari. I know we have no future but she is my first true love. Fatima has always been a friend and companion. I can die for Pari.

When Pari leaned to whisper to him in the shah's palace, he was tempted to hug her, smell her, taste her. But he knew the risks. *She is such a tease.* Isa smiled as he thought about Pari's flirtatious behaviour. *I wish she could come home with me. But this is blasphemy; moreover, my sasurji is here to escort me to Bengal.*

The contradictions had been exacerbated in Isa's mind after a rendezvous with his mates in the Safavid army. His friends were now enjoying a life of debauchery, bedding nautch girls and prostitutes, and indulging themselves every which way. Witnessing the unbridled passion between the girls and the soldiers made Isa feel like an intruder, and deeply lonely.

I too want to enjoy the moment and live my life in full, he reflected as he walked towards Kolah Farangi. He made sure he walked through the boulevard so that no one could indict him for spying. When he spotted Pari approaching him through the bushes, Isa hastily looked around, adroitly jumped over the hedgerow and fervently kissed the love of his life behind the bushes.

The kiss was long, intense and passionate, as if they were sucking a lifetime of separation. Isa gazed into her deep dark eyes, and crooned, "Dark is the night, darker your eyes; sweet are your kisses, sweeter your eyes!"

"You love my *aankhen* more than my kisses!"

"I know not what is true, Pari. I only know I love you, and without you, nothing is true!"

Pari had never seen Isa be so poetic though she basked in his adulation.

"I can see you are practising your speech for your begum on me! And pray, when were you planning to tell me that you were married?"

Isa let out a long sigh.

"She is my *mauseri behen.* We grew up together. She can never ignite the passion inside me. I have never been in love with Fatima and never will be. It is you who makes my *dil ki dhadkan* go fast. The thought of lying in your arms has kept me alive in the prison. And tonight, I madly want to make love to you."

Isa swiftly caught Pari's soft delicate hand and first held it gently next to his heart, beating wildy, and then brought it down so that she could feel his manhood, throbbing lustily.

Pari gave out a loud sigh.

"We are sailing in the same boat, Isk. Even I am married to my cousin. I like him but I try to stay away from him because whenever he makes love to me, I feel no love or passion and close my eyes to imagine you. I too long for your *muhabbat* and we cannot let this night go to waste. Come upstairs with me, Isk. Quick!"

"But Pari, surely that is a great risk for both of us. We might get caught."

"Isn't life about taking risks? Fear not, for I exited from the backstairs, while my room is latched from inside. Come Isk. Time is running out!"

As the couple darted towards Kolah Farangi, Isa noticed it had corner porticos like the Ali Qapu palace. They almost flew through one of the rear entrances, moved across the hall and into a corner room, from where they ascended a curved staircase.

They stepped into a patio and Pari pulled Isa into a corner room, silently latched the door and then ushered him into a spacious room. "Welcome to my abode!"

Isa took in the beauty of the room, mouth agape. The ornate pillars and arched windows, the large bed positioned at the centre, with tables, chairs and sofas discreetly placed at various corners of the chamber highlighted Pari's taste and sophistication. Without further ado, Isa smooched Pari deeply and fiercely. While their tongues played with each other, he reached out to undress her. Before Pari could realise, her gown was lying on the floor and she was left standing in her chemise. She blushed and backstepped towards the middle of the hall, but that only accentuated her silhouette against the moonlight.

Pari's curvaceous body heightened the passion within Isa. He was now a man possessed. He gently embraced Pari and murmered, "Pari, I have been dreaming of this night ever since I met you."

Isa quickly bundled her in his strong arms and tenderly carried her to the bed.

"Allow me to appreciate Allah's gift," said Isa huskily as he started removing her chemise.

"It's not fair. I too want to see you in flesh."

"Jo hukum, Shehzadi!"

He quickly took off his garments and lay down next to her.

"Isk, you are still wearing your *langot*! Not fair!"

She bent down, swiftly removed it and clutched Isa's throbbing manhood. Her touch set Isa into throes of passion and he started leaving love bites on her back and shoulders.

As he kissed Pari behind the ears, bit on her ear lobes, she moaned loudly.

He then shifted his attention to her rosy cheeks, full lips and firm breasts.

While his one hand kneaded one of her breasts, his eager mouth sucked hard on the other. Isa remarked, "Jaan, I could suck them for eternity. And nibble on these cherries forever." Meanwhile, Pari was trying to guide Isa's manhood inside her. As Isa gently entered her, she purred, "Isk, since your *jaan* and *jahan* are here, why return?"

Isa could not answer, for paroxysm after paroxysm of passion engulfed them, and as Pari cried out, Isa ejaculated a lifetime reserve of desire into her.

As they locked eyes, Isa said, "Jaan, I would have loved to stay back but both of us are married to different people. We know that my staying here now is an impossibility, so let me return. I will be back when I can claim you!"

Isa slid down to feast on her breasts, and as he started going further down his feet touched a metallic object which dropped on the floor and sent out a reverberating sound.

Pari leapt out of the bed to retrieve her ghungroo.

"I had removed my ghungroos so that my movements could not be heard."

"Let me put them back on your lovely legs."

As he caressed her ankle, attempting to tie the ghungroos back, Isa said, "I remember how these ghungroos resonated when you walked. I want to hear them when we meet next to take you with me forever."

"For that Isk, my shohar has to die!"

Pari then hesitated, wickedly smiled and boldly asked, "*Mere mehboob*, do you have any suggestions for eliminating him?"

"Slow poisoning is probably the easiest and most effective way. A daily morning dose of *poust* will send anyone to the grave."

Isa winked.

Pari looked at him in admiration.

"What is poust?"

"It is a drink of raw opium made from soaking poppy seeds overnight in water."

Dawn was near, and the two lovers had only a few fleeting moments before bidding farewell, so they made the most of that Muharram night and continued to passionately make love to each other, hoping the night would stay young.

9

A Moment of Revelation

AD 1576

"Sridhara, you appear tense and worried and there are dark circles under your eyes. You need rest. Why do you not just relax here for tomorrow and proceed the day after? Surely, the Mughals are not going to attack your bastion on the Rajmahal hills tomorrow!"

Bhikam pensively looked at Sridhara while sipping on his *dheno*.

Sridhara, the commander of the Karrani army, had just returned to Tanda after the Battle of Rajmahal where the Mughals and Daud Khan Karrani's army were locked in a battle for the last four months. Monsoon had now set upon the lower Gangetic plains and soon the countryside would be flooded. Daud had been informed that Emperor Akbar had sent word for reinforcements. The decisive attack would happen over the next few days. Sridhara wasted no time and had rushed to the capital in Tanda for securing additional horsemen, provisions and ammunition.

Tanda was twenty four kilometres downstream on the Ganga from the Rajmahal hills and lay opposite Gaur across the river. Sulaiman Karrani, the father of Daud Khan, had shifted the capital there from Gaur due to its mint town status. It took Sridhara only two hours to reach the capital. He managed to assemble two thousand cavalry men and despatched them to Rajmahal and left instructions for the armoury to be loaded into boats and start their journey at midnight.

Sridhara would depart for the battlefield early next morning and now relaxed at his terrace overlooking the Ganga with his brothers Bhikam Roy and Basanta Roy. The eldest brother Bhikam maintained the accounts of the sultanate and the youngest supervised their zamindari.

Bhikam urged Sridhara again, "Why do you need to leave tomorrow? Stay back for a few more days!"

Sridhara shrugged.

"Dada, Daud's overambitiousness and his retinue of sycophants have made him *ahankari* and mistrustful. You know I have tried to reason with him in the past on the need for consolidation and building up one's defence before opposing, but he has ignored my advice. If I do not go tomorrow, he will start questioning my actions."

Saying so, Sridhara took a puff of the hookah.

Basanta looked at his brothers askance and said, "Surely, the sultan should resist the Mughal onslaught!"

Bhikam smiled and said, "Basanta, when Sulaiman ascended the throne on the death of his brother Taj, he acknowledged the supremacy of Akbar and did not assert his independence, for he needed to develop his revenue base and strengthen his soldiery. Remember, Sher Shah Suri who started as a commander in Babar's army, also consolidated his position in the east for over six years before challenging Humayun."

"Exactly," said Sridhara. "Sulaiman even ensured that the mosques announce Akbar's name in the *jummah khutbah* to maintain peace while he continued to extend his territory towards the south and north-east. This is the hallmark of the wise and shrewd ruler. Unfortunately, he died before he could give wings to his dream."

"Yes," added Bhikam, "when Sulaiman expired, his eldest son Bayazid became the emperor. He believed the Mughals could as easily be overthrown as the Utkals, and he therefore immediately declared his *azadi*. His ego made him announce his name to be read during the jummah khutbah and he even started issuing coins in his own name. When his well-wishers advised him against the same, they were expelled from the kingdom. We all knew that Bayazid had chosen a suicidal path and were relieved when his cousin assassinated him."

Sridhara took another drag of the hookah and refilled his tumbler with dheno. Typically, it was unthinkable in Bengali Hindu society for a younger brother to drink with his elder brother, but the Guha clan of Jessore owed their prosperity to Sridhara, because of whom they had earned the honorific title Roy, and therefore accepted his transgressions.

"Sulaiman once confessed to me how they were almost obliterated when they asserted their independency following the death of Islam Shah Suri. Overpowered by Hemu, they had to flee the battlefield. Akbar's invasion of Delhi was a blessing in disguise for the Karranis as Hemu met his end at the Battle of Panipat. That provided the Karrani dynasty the necessary respite to consolidate but also a timely remonstration never to rush to declare one's sovereignty.

"Dada, these young usurpers do not know their history. You know, when the well-meaning Afghan lords were banished by Bayazid for advising him to maintain peace, I requested Kalapahad to pursue the emperor not to challenge the Mughals."

"*Mejda,* how could you trust Kalapahad? He destroyed our Hindu temples in Konark, Puri and Kamakhya."

Sridhara smiled.

"Kalapahad was born Rajib Lochan Ray, a Brahmin who became the commander of King Gajapati Mukunda Deva's army. He fell in love with Sulaiman's daughter Gulnaaz and converted to Islam only to marry her. In those tumultuous days, Rajib often approached me for counsel."

Basanta exclaimed, "That's incredulous! Where did Rajib meet Gulnaaz?"

"This is like peeling the onion and it will take days to recount. Suffice it is to say that Sulaiman knew that Kalinga could not be captured with Kalapahad around and invited Rajib to Tanda to befriend him. It was love at first sight for Rajib when he met Gulnaaz and converted to Islam and adopted the name Muhammad Farmuli to marry the princess. This way Sulaiman killed two stones with one bird—Mukunda Deva refused to have a Muslim as his army commander and Kalapahad became the general of Sulaiman's army!"

"Why was he called Kalapahad, Dada?"

Sridhara was bemused.

"Rajib was a giant of a man, but not so dark in colour to be called Kalapahad. He got the sobriquet because of his perceived darkness of character, which stemmed from his actions that were harsh and detrimental to the Hindus.

"But who am I to talk about this? I have also done so many heinious things for Daud. I have assassinated quite a few for no fault of theirs, but only because Daud thought they may be conspirators. I still shudder whenever I recollect Daud ordering me to eliminate his wazir. May his soul rest in peace. Ishwar will not forgive me and will punish me for my past crimes. After all, *jemon karma temni phol* (as you sow, so shall you reap). I have at least ensured I will not be murdered by my son."

Sighing, Sridhara stared at the thunderous dark monsoon clouds, hoping their evening get-together would not be disrupted by a sudden downpour.

Basanta still had a lot of questions.

"But Dada, three years ago, you were on the verge of victory against the Mughals. Surely you can repeat that!"

Sridhara nodded.

"Yes, Munim Khan, along with Todar Mal and Man Singh, attacked us in Hajipur while Daud retreated across the river to Pataliputra. We knew it was a do-or-die battle and it was thus inconclusive, but last year we were defeated in the Battle of Tukaroi by the Mughals, and we had to retreat to Kalinga as Munim captured Tanda. That should give you an indication of their strength. Unfortunately, Munim died of plague in October and Daud returned to capture Bengal. Now the Mughals have cornered us again and this time in Rajmahal. There is no escape for us."

Basanta persisted, "You all will roar back. I am confident victory will be yours. What I do not understand is why are all the Rajputs and Khatris, like Man Singh and Raja Todar Mal, siding with Akbar?"

Before Sridhara could respond, Bhikam intervened, "Sulaiman once told me that Todar Mal began his career as a writer under Sher Shah and after the defeat of the Suris, shifted to Delhi. Bairam Khan, the regent of Akbar, was slowly poisoning the emperor which Todar came to know through his mistress who was employed as a maid in Bairam's household. Todar went and informed Niyamat, the chief *napunsak* of Akbar's harem, and Akbar in gratitude employed Todar. Akbar was impressed by his loyalty and started employing more Hindus. I have heard that Akbar has over a dozen wives and a few thousand women in his harem, but while he enjoys with them, he only sleeps in the bed of his Hindu begum Mariam!"

Then turning to Sridhara, Bhikam asked, "Yes, you lost the Battle of Tukaroi and Daud had to sign the Treaty of Kataka by which he ceded Bengal and Bihar and retained only Kalinga, but your *sena* had the upper hand till your commander Gujar Khan fell. So why are you so despondent now?"

Sridhara sighed.

"It is difficult to maintain the morale of an army when you are always being defeated. Also, we realised that given the strength of the Mughal army, our success lies in catching them unawares.

"During Sulaiman's rule, Daud commanded an army of over forty thousand cavalry, four thousand elephants, one-and-a-half lakh infantry and two hundred cannons. But over the last four years, our strength has diminished and now our army is less than half of that. Further, there is no longer any element of surprise, and we are sitting ducks on the Rajmahal hills. No Dada, I have a premonition the end is near, and the Mughals will spare none to squash the Afghan resistance forever!"

"Your disquiet is correct. I am sorry that we are having this conversation now when we should have had it long ago. Since you have been frustrated for a long time, why have you not resigned from your position?"

"Dada, these prodigal rulers are vindictive and lack wisdom. Daud not only eliminated his wazir, but also confiscated all his *sampatti*! I was worried my resignation would be viewed as a sign of rebellion and along with me, Daud would eliminate all of us and loot Jessore."

Tears rolled down Bhikam's eyes as he embraced his brother.

"Thank you for your magnificence and selflessness, bhai."

Sridhara gulped the last peg of dheno and murmured, "Ah, this rice brew has really refreshed me. Chanakya was so right when he said that it is important to determine the location of the brewery before building a castle or fort, for that is the surest way to a man's heart! Now for some *machh bhaat* and a nice sleep because having biriyani every day at the camp is boring."

But as he got up to proceed for dinner, he said, "Dada, Basanta, please come downstairs with me. I have something important to show you."

Sridhara led them to his large iron chest. He opened the chest and announced, "The list of all the treasuries of the empire is here. As also whatever wealth remains of the Karrani Empire. Please safeguard them and do not let them fall into the hands of the Mughals. If we succumb, carry them to Jessore. The monsoon is coming, and it will protect you."

"Since you say the end is near, stay back here for a few days. We will spread the news that you are sick so that you have a ready excuse should Daud question you. If Daud falls, we can all return to our beloved Jessore."

"Dada, ever since I killed my son, I cannot look at my *stree*'s face. The guilt troubles me and returning to my family would haunt me more. Let me go and fight, and let it be God's will should I die!"

"Dada, I did not keep my word!"

Sridhara was puzzled.

"What do you mean, Basanta?"

Basanta, with his eyes down, stammered, "Your son is alive and well. He is a handsome boy now and his wedding is fixed for next month!"

10

The Bhoumik of Sarail

"ABBU, WHAT ARE YOU DOING upstairs alone?"

Musa came up from the cabin to join Isa at the deck.

"I am enjoying the surroundings, Beta!"

It was the month of Ograhayon. Autumn was already over. Sitting on the deck of his bajra, Isa scanned the surroundings. There was water everywhere. When the monsoon arrived in Ashar, the mighty Meghna burst at its seams and engulfed the countryside. That was almost five months ago. The rains had now stopped for nearly three months, but the fields were still inundated. It was difficult to say where the river ended and the land began, but for the protruding trees and the crops. The colour of the paddy fields metamorphosised from a translucent green to a vibrant yellow. Sarail resembled a gold mine as the crop glittered under the morning rays of the sun. Isa knew the villagers had to stay alert to protect the crops from being looted.

"But there is nothing to see except *pani* all around! Practise sword fighting with me instead?"

"Good suggestion, but the floor is wet and you may slip and hurt yourself!"

Musa noticed the moist floor and enquired, "Why is the floor *gila*? Has it been raining again?"

Isa looked at his firstborn. He was almost ten now. Everyone said Musa was Isa's replica. The kajal under Musa's eyes accentuated his sharp penetrating eyes. Musa reminded Isa of Ismail very much. *The same lanky physique, copper skin tone, inquisitiveness and innocence* ... Isa's thoughts trailed off.

"Do not worry, rains will come again during the summer *kalbaisakhi*. This is *shishir*—the dew heralds that Poush is near."

Winter was Isa's favourite season as the weather gave the country folks the much needed relief from the hot wet climate. It was the season for harvesting and the most auspicious month for Hindus. Isa briefly wondered, *Why Bengali Hindus never marry in Poush when it is such an auspicious month*? Looking at Musa, he thought, *Soon I have to look for a bride for him. I want Musa to select his own bride when he becomes an adult. I do not want him to suffer a loveless marriage like mine.*

While it was true that Muslims could have four wives, in rural Bengal, having even two wives was frowned upon.

It had been over a decade since Isa had returned home, yet he still dreamt of Pari. When he was awake and in his senses, he never felt like romancing Fatima but at night when he was sleeping, he would often imagine Pari next to him, and make wild love to his bibi and always call out Pari's name in throes of passion. That was how Musa was conceived, but now, Fatima would gently move his arms away. She has realised that Isa was never really hers, and she had made peace with the bitter truth.

If only Pari was here with me... Isa's train of thought was interrupted as Musa impatiently asked, "Abbu, what are you thinking?"

Isa smiled.

"I was thinking whom to select for your bride, Musa. What kind of a girl would you like to marry?"

Musa was caught unawares, his face reddened and he scurried downstairs to the cabin.

Isa laughed and turned his attention to the surroundings again. It was evident that this year would yield a bumper crop. Villagers would be celebrating the harvest, but Isa knew they had to be careful as the Mogs and the Portuguese had been reconnoitring the area for the last couple of years to plunder the new-found prosperity of Sarail. Now, with winter setting in on the plains of Bengal, the water on the fields would recede and the foreigners were aware that this was an opportune time to loot the harvest.

Isa secretly congratulated himself for Sarail's renewed prosperity. When he had returned from captivity to Bengal, Ramdas pleaded with Sulaiman Karrani to hand Isa the zamindari of Sarail.

Ramdas reasoned, "Sultan, eastern Bengal was the granary for the sultanate, but frequent raids from the Mogs and the Portuguese have led to loss of revenue. The strong zamindars of Sripur and Chandradwip protected the region from southern invasions and hence it was from the east that the attacks now happened. There is a need to put up a resistance in the east and I strongly believe Isa would be the ideal leader for that region since his late father ruled from there. Isa is familiar with the place, its problems and peculiarities."

The sultan saw the merit of Ramdas's justification and made Isa the bhowmik of Sarail.

Isa was thrilled when he was appointed as a bhuiyan.

How I longed for Sarail in Turan, he thought wistfully. Yet, when he arrived there, he was shocked to see his village lay in ruins. It hardly resembled the place he had grown up as a boy. He was most despondent when he saw their family mansion in ruins.

Isa reflected, *For Sarail to prosper, her people need to return, and I have to ensure peace and protection by maintaining an army.* Yet, this was a chicken and egg situation for funds were required to maintain an army and if people did not return first and create the revenues, he could not deploy forces. After much procrastination, Isa finally addressed the problem by creating clearings in the forest and encouraging artisans to return and set up their dwellings within the cleared area of the forest. The forest barricade was fortified with bamboo shields and tied with jute ropes so that wild animals could not attack the inhabitants. One could reach the enclosure only by walking through the forest for which an intimate knowledge of the landscape was essential. By setting up habitation within the forest, Isa ensured temporary respite from the marauders and the much-needed breather to organise his defences.

Isa identified a few locals and trained them in warfare, and together they escorted the artisans to Sonargaon for selling their wares. This was essential to ensure that the folks were not waylaid by bandits on their way back to the village. The ensuing sustenance attracted more natives to return to Sarail which entailed more clearing of forest lands. As forest lands continued to be cleared, Isa and his men dug a deep moat across the edge of the forest from where they accessed the Meghna, which could only be crossed through drawbridges, and which were removed during the night. He had standing instructions that the bridges had to be withdrawn at the sign of any stranger and guards were deployed throughout the day for lookout. In case the drawbridges were withdrawn, the stranded villagers had to seek shelter elsewhere immediately.

The strategy had worked well and people had prospered, and within a few years, farming was also initiated beyond the forests. Isa now maintained an army of five thousand men. He would often think, *How I wish to build my mansion in the open but doing that would expose me to the enemies. Sarail does not enjoy the natural barriers like Sripur or Sonargaon. It is vulnerable to attacks.*

The forests provided the only fortification against the raiders, and thus, Isa had strict instructions that thick vegetation be maintained all around their village so that it was difficult to identify their location. The trees would also provide the first line of defence against cannons. However, the crops had attracted attention, and he was aware that enquires were being made to identify their location.

I am sure an attack from the Mogs and the Harmads is imminent.

Isa was a worried man for another reason too. Though the monsoon was over, dark clouds were gathering in the horizon. The Karranis had been routed at the Battle of Rajmahal over four months ago and Daud and his men were mercilessly slaughtered by the Mughal army. Even Sridhara had fallen in that battle. The Mughals had now established their suzerainty in Bengal. Emperor Akbar now oversaw the province through his subahdar Khan Jahan and Isa was aware that the Mughals were now trying to subjugate the Afghan warlords to stifle all mutinies in Bengal.

Isa had gathered that the Mughals were planning to introduce a new revenue system in Bengal where the land would be measured in bighas, equivalent to fourteen thousand and four hundred square feet, and classified into four different categories—from being the most fertile to fallow land. Further, each category would be sub-classified into three classes based on the quality of the crop. The Bengal administration had now initiated surveys to estimate the average produce of different crops over the last decade so that revenue estimation was no longer arbitrary and zamindars had to necessarily pay one-third of the revenue estimate as taxes.

Isa also understood that while this system was being rolled out, land revenue would be imposed on lands which had not yet been surveyed. Isa felt that the system was arbitrary since the revenue was based on the average collection of the last decade and planned to oppose it since his uncle Ramdas had unscrupulously inflated his revenue figures in the past so that Isa could be in the good books of the Karranis. Now, that same benevolence would be a hindrance and Isa would need to pay a higher tax than justified.

Isa, however, was relieved on one account. Bhikam and Basanta had absconded on the fall of Tanda and had retreated to the interiors of Khulna with all the wealth and tax records. He became aware of this recently when he had travelled to Jessore to attend the wedding ceremony of Sridhara's son Pratapaditya. The wedding gave him the opportunity to meet the leading bhuiyans of Bengal—Mukundaram Roy of Bhushna, Raja Lakshman Manikhya of Bhuluya, Fazl Ghazi of Bhawal, Chand Ghazi of Chandpratap and Raja Kangsanarayan Laskar Roy of Taharpur. Both the Ghazis had immediately warmed up to him and looked upon a descendant from the Hussain Shah family as their natural leader. But most of the zamindars were Hindus and they looked at Isa with disdain.

Isa pondered as he stood on the deck, *I have an arduous task of gaining their trust if we have to be united. Because, without unity, this land would be divided and fall like a pack of cards under the Mughal invasion.*

Ramdas had impressed upon Isa the importance of Chand Roy and Jagadanda Roy as valued confederates. Yet, Isa could gauge that Chand Roy was now past his prime and valued the judgement of Kedar Roy—a stripling—rather than his own opinion. One day a chance encounter with Kandarpanarayan Roy corroborated his opinion about Chand Roy.

Kandarpanarayan said, "Isa, I must tell you that Chand is a changed man ever since his only daughter Sona became a widow. It seems the entire community wanted her to perform sati, but Chand's love for his daughter had prevailed and he had been able to protect her from being cremated along with his *damad.* This had resulted in Chand's loss of stature as a leading Kayastha among the orthodox Hindus and Chand now contents himself in seeking solace by worshipping Goddess Tara."

The heat was getting intense on the deck, so Isa moved downstairs to the cabin.

As he entered the cabin of the bajra, Fatima announced, "Musa tells me that you are searching for his bride? His cousin would be the ideal wife for him."

Fatima was dressed in a green salwar-kurta, and not wearing the burqa. She had a rotund face, fair complexion, thick black eyelashes and dark eyes, a slightly plump figure and medium height.

"Fatima, I don't understand why we Mussalmans marry only our cousins! I want our son to marry when he is old enough to make his choices. I was only teasing him!"

Fatima smiled.

"Your mission has been successful."

Isa let out a loud sigh. A worried expression clouded his face.

"Something is troubling you?"

Isa nodded.

"It is the time for harvest, and I fear attacks from all fronts—the Mogs, the Mughals and the Harmads. I worry about Musa. I don't want him to be enslaved as I was. The times are not good, and while I have tried to build a strong defence, Sarail is too exposed."

"So what do you propose to do about it?"

Isa reflected.

"I want the two of you to shift to Sonargaon."

"Are you planning to bring Pari here when I leave?"

Isa was stunned.

"How do you know about her?"

Fatima smiled.

"You keep on murmuring her name in your sleep."

Isa sheepishly grinned.

"I am sorry ... Pari was someone who gave me solace when I had lost all hope in life back when I was a slave."

Fatima chose not to respond. Theirs was a marriage of convenience now.

But then Isa turned serious.

"I cannot resist the Mughal army with my current force. I need to develop alliance with powerful rulers to combat Akbar. Maybe I will go to the Tipperah kingdom and join their army—I have heard they have employed quite a few Afghans as their army commanders. But I plan to shift my kingdom to Sonargaon soon, once I am a force to reckon with; and in the meantime, I will be mentally at peace if both of you stay in Sonargaon for I know the two of you will be safe in your Abbu's khanqah."

11

The Letter

"*Uff, what happened*?" Isa wondered.

The morning commotion awoke him. He loathed to get up. It had been two years since Fatima and Musa left for Sonargaon. Now that he lived alone, he enjoyed late nights, drinking dheno alone and gazing at the stars. He would have blissfully turned the other side and gone back to his rather naughty dreams, but shouts of "call sardar" stirred him up from his deep sleep. Reluctantly, he arose and dressed, taking caution to gargle with rosewater and sprinkle a generous dose of attar on himself to hide the odour of alcohol. He stepped out of his four-room hut and saw villagers patiently waiting outside for him. Rakhal, one of the sentinels, rushed to him and cried out, "Jamidar babu, we are being attacked by *rakshasas*!"

Isa looked at Rakhal with disbelief.

"Do they even exist?" Isa asked.

Isa knew about Lord Rama's struggles with Ravana, the king of the rakshasas.

But that was an epic.

"How much did you drink last night?"

Rakhal was shocked and dismayed.

"What are you saying, Kartamashai? I was keeping an eye on the surroundings from a treetop, watching for any unexpected activity, when I saw a group of black people approach our forest. They are as black as coal—I have never seen people like that! I tell you they are rakshasas. There is even a Ghatotkacha among them. I was so frightened ...I immediately raised the drawbridge and ran here!"

The mention of dark people reminded Isa of the Kaka Siahs, the black slaves from Africa who were engaged across Turan as soldiers and servants, though Pari called them Hajis since most slaves were caught after performing Hajj.

Are these people from Qazvin? He rubbed his chin as he thought.

Suddenly, Isa's face lit up. He had heard the news that Shah Tahmasp had died and thus these strangers were probably sent by Pari. He smiled at Rakhal. "I am sure there is some other explanation. Rakshasas do not live any more. Is it not true that your Lord Rama vanquished all the demons?"

Saying so, Isa hurried to the drawbridge.

"Ah!" he uttered with great relief.

Isa spotted Ikram among the visitors although he looked slightly dejected. Even the shah's personal bodyguard—Masood—whom Rakhal had identified as Ghatotkacha, was there. The men were all Habashis as the shah preferred to engage Ethiopian eunuchs as servants for their skills in warfare.

"*Khush Amdeed.* How are things in Qazvin?"

Ikram's shoulders drooped.

Isa was puzzled.

He hestatingly asked, "How is everyone Ikram?"

Without replying, Ikram handed Isa a sealed document.

Isa immediately recognised Pari's seal. He was elated. He hastily opened the packet and found a letter from her. As Isa opened it, he noted the date. The letter was written around two months ago.

> *Mere* Isk,
>
> If you are reading this letter, it means I have failed you in love. My bags are packed and I have sent them in advance with Ikram and a few of my trusted servants. I plan to follow them later in the night, after I have gone and received Shah Mohammad Khodabanda and Khayr—you remember, you had met my half-brother and his wife at your last dinner in Qazvin. The Kizilbash chieftains had pleaded with me to run the empire after I had turned down the offer of the crown, and they ordained that Mohammad could be the titular head, but I had to be the de facto power if Qazvin were to prosper. I accepted their terms but had planned to abscond to Bengal to your loving arms under the pretext of visiting Mecca in this holy month of the pilgrimage. But Mohammad and Khayr have relocated from Shiraz to Qazvin today. I was not expecting their visit.

I smell a conspiracy. Khayr has started calling herself Mahd-e Olya, the highest-ranking cradle, which means she has garnered the support of some of the Kizilbash clans. I plan to have five thousand guards around me during today's reception ceremony, so that I am well protected, and after the ceremony announce my departure for Mecca. Ikram and the advance party will wait for me in the Alborz Mountains, somewhere near the Alamut Castle where you had been imprisoned. I will make a detour and hope to join them there!

I strongly believe that like Iltutmish, you too will become the shahenshah of Hindustan. But after our eventful night which shall ever be ensconced in my memory, I have been lonely and longing for you. You keep on appearing in my dreams. I wanted to end my loveless marriage so that I could unite with you, but Badi-al never visited me since. I believe he was smitten by a courtesan. Badi-al is no more and may his soul rest in peace, but more on that later.

I regret being born a woman in a society where we are looked down upon and exist only for sexual gratification for the menfolk. A Shia man is allowed to marry four times, my father had nine wives and innumerable concubines, but we women can only belong to one person. Age-old beliefs cannot be easily converted. I had tried my best to make a difference for women in Islamic society, but now I am saddened by the myopic vision of men in power and do not aspire for anything apart from being with you, my love.

You know, I was inspired by Razia Sultana and wanted to be an empress like her. But I have been disillusioned with the politics of the Safavid court which is complex and controlled by the Kizilbash. I was under the impression that my father had successfully neutralised their influence over the last fifty years, but once he fell ill four years back, I was surprised to see the Kizilbash effortlessly regain their control. I feel my father's reluctance to name his successor fuelled the insecurities of the various claimants and they turned to the Kizilbash to chart their advancement.

Abbu was only ten years old when he became the emperor, and he ruled the next few years under the influence of the Kizilbash, but I wonder why he did not reduce their authority and power in the court when they were responsible for the civil war that erupted in the early years of his reign. Although Abbu did mention once that he should have eliminated all the Kizilbash, but he was helpless as he needed their help to fight the Uzbeks and the Ottomans.

Abbu also mentioned that to curb the power of the Kizilbash, he encouraged the recruitment of military slaves who could be employed as ghilman and fully loyal to the shah. I am fortunate that he started this practice because that is how I came to meet you!

Abbu believed the Kizilbash had powerful support in his harem and any action against them would jeopardise his life. Thinking of his remark now as I pen this letter, I am amazed by my father's astuteness.

My mother was the favourite of the emperor, yet it was the children from his first wife Sultanum Begum who emerged as the leading contenders for the throne. Her son Mohammad Khodabanda, being nearly blind, was overlooked and the two key aspirants were my half-brothers Ismail Mirza Safavi, locked in Qahqaheh castle, and Haydar Mirza Safavi. I knew Haydar could not be trusted but did not voice my opinion.

While the succession battle was gaining prominence, Abbu expressed his desire to make me the empress. I reminded him that the court officials would never accept a person from the opposite sex as the emperor. Abbu then suggested that I could be the Mahd-e Olya with Badi-al as the titular emperor, but I impressed upon Abbu that his nephew Ibrahim would make a far superior ruler. I could see the displeasure on his face, but he did not know the pangs of my heart, that now I only longed for you. Unfortunately, Abbu expired two years ago without announcing a successor and I have a strong suspicion that Haydar poisoned him!

I was aghast when Haydar proclaimed himself emperor on the death of Abbu. No meetings were conducted between the Kizilbash officials to nominate the next leader, and I knew swift action had to be taken to neutralise Haydar or else many innocent lives would be lost. I immediately ensured that the Kizilbash guards protecting the palace were from clans supporting my other half-brother Ismail. I could not canvas for Sulaiman as most nobles believed that the empire should not pass on to a Circassian descent (as you know, my mother was a Circassian). Haydar quickly got me arrested. I had to prostrate naked in front of him to convince him of my loyalty, while he pinched my breasts, kicked my rear and mocked at my nakedness. What a perverted soul!

I wept and promised to convince Ismail, my brothers and other influential people to accept his sovereignty. Haydar gloated over my vulnerability and finally released me, ordering me to leave the mahal, but I could not let such a badmash go unpunished.

I have a duplicate set of keys for the palace from Abbu's time, and which Haydar was unaware of, which I now passed on to my uncle Shamkhal who opened a rear entrance for the troops to come in and Haydar, in desperation, hid in the harem masquerading as a woman. As soldiers started searching every nook and corner of the palace for Haydar, words reached his supporters, and they stormed towards the palace. But Shamkhal had already closed the rear entrance. Meanwhile, Haydar was spotted and beheaded, and his torso thrown to his troops. Thus, Haydar ruled for less than a day. Allah is great.

With Haydar assassinated, I called a meeting of the Kizilbash chieftains and mentioned that Shah Tahmasp had suggested Ibrahim as the next shah. But all the officials were of the opinion that Ismail should be the emperor. I recalled father's admiration for Ismail in the wars against the Ottomans and relented. I personally ensured he was announced as the new shah of the Safavid dynasty, hoping he could consolidate the Safavid dynasty while I retreated to my nest in Bengal.

You should think that after all I did for Ismail, he would be grateful to me. Instead, he turned out to be a *ghaddar*. Probably, his long stint in jail had affected him and made him mentally unstable. Ismail started executing all his brothers and other royal princes so that there were no challengers to the throne. He even strangled my bhai Suleiman and followed it up by killing Badi-al and his brother Ibrahim. He probably spared Mohammad Khodabanda because he was blind and old and stayed in distant Shiraz.

Wanting to be the sole authority, Ismail kept me under house arrest and forbade the Kizilbash or any other officials to meet me at Kolah Farangi. He withdrew my guards and attendants, instructed that I could not set foot outside the Chahar Bagh gardens and treated me with disdain whenever we met. He also started sympathising with the Sunnis which antagonised the Kizilbash. Seeing Ismail's callous and arrogant leadership, I realised his rule had to end. I plotted his downfall.

Your directions came in handy. I slowly started poisoning him with opium water in his morning drink which I administered through his concubines, and I was successful in my mission when four months back, he suddenly collapsed and died on the spot. I am sure the Kizilbash suspected my handiwork, but everyone was glad that Ismail was gone. In his one year of rule, he had depleted the treasury and the Kizilbash now begged me to be their ruler.

Ismail had eliminated most male claimants, except for his children and that ofhis elder bother Mohammad Khodabanda and his descendants. The Kizilbash were reluctant to put Shoja al-Din Mohammad Safavi—the eight-month-old son of Ismail—as the emperor as they were sure the various clans would start fighting for his regency. Hence, they proposed Mohammad Khodabanda's name, but knowing he was old, wasted and profligate, they requested that Mohammad be the titular head while I run the empire. I had to accept their proposition. But the Kizilbash are now circling on me like vultures. I have a premonition that Khayr's arrival means that my end is near. I will take my chances but hope Allah is with me.

You know I had promised you that the next time we meet, you would hear the echoes of my ghungroos. There would be nothing illicit about this meeting. I have packed my ghungroos with Ikram, but I plan to wear them when I catch up with you. If you see Ikram handing the ghungroos to you, you must know that I have failed you in your ishq!

Isa finished reading the letter, marvelled at Pari's composition and asked, "Where is Princess Pari?"

Silently, Ikram handed Isa the ghungroos, while Masood added, "While our princess was planning to exit the city, she was encircled and called back to the mahal for some strategic discussions. She volunteered, but as soon as she entered the palace, she was strangled to death. Khayr had a hand in this. Shamkhal and Ismail's son were beheaded shortly."

Isa's face went blank in shock and grief.

12

The Pact

"MAHARAJA AMAR DEBBARMAN MANIKYA, THE ruler of Tipperah, the one hundred and fortieth descendant of the Chandravansha dynasty, is entering the court!" the drummers announced.

All court officials and visitors, including Isa, arose.

It was the end of summer of the year 1578. Isa was in the court of the maharaj of Tipperah, an independent kingdom in the hilly region of south-east Bengal.

Isa turned to Kandarpanarayan Roy and asked, "Surely, the Manikya dynasty cannot be ruling for such a long time. If we assume four generations to account for each century, it means that the Chandravansha dynasty has been ruling Tipperah for the last three thousand and five hundred years. This is fascinating!"

Kandarpanarayan grinned at Isa. Over the last couple of years, the two had developed a friendship and a relationship of trust which was unthinkable between Muslim and Hindu zamindars. Both had realised that for their regions to prosper, maintaining peace and stability in Bengal was paramount, and they, along with Kedar Roy of Sripur, had collaborated to protect the region from the marauders.

Kandarpanarayan replied, "I have studied our family *itihas*. There is no mention of the Tipperah kingdom during my ancestor Danujmardan's reign in Chandradwip. The first reference we have of this kingdom in our chronicles is less than two hundred years ago when it is mentioned that Maha Manikya declared himself the *samrat* of Tipperah."

"Yes, the drummers mentioned the ancestry, not their years of reign in Tipperah. It might be they migrated eastwards to protect themselves from the Huns, but the Chandravansha dynasty has a prestigious ancestry. Reminds me of how my sasur keeps reciting his genealogy to ascertain his nobility!"

Kandarpanarayan nodded.

"You are right. Yayati, the founder of the Chandravansha dynasty, is supposed to be the grandson of Lord Shiva and Goddess Parvati. Lord Krishna was a descendant of the Chandravansha dynasty. We are all gathered here in Udaipur, which is one of the Shakti peethas in the subcontinent. What a coincidence."

Noticing Isa's bewildering look, Kedar Roy, the scion of Sripur, who was sitting next to them and enjoying their conversation teased Isa, "My father and brother Chand Roy tell me that your *pitaji* Kalidas was a staunch Hindu. Yet, he embraced Islam and not imparted any knowledge of our rich Hindu heritage to you. Don't you know about Brahma our creator, Vishnu the preserver and Shiva the destroyer?"

Isa looked sheepish.

"Brahma, to create the universe, performed a yagna, to please Shiva and his feminine counterpart Shakti. Once the universe was created, Brahma's son Daksha performed several yagnas to obtain Shakti as his daughter Sati. Sati wanted to marry Shiva, but Daksha was against the marriage as he considered Shiva uncouth. Sati nevertheless married Shiva.

"Sometime later, her father performed a magnificent yagna where he invited everyone he could except his daughter and son-in-law. An intrigued Sati went to witness the yagna, but noticing her father's deep contempt for her beloved, self-immolated herself.

"The grief-striken Shiva lifted Sati's corpse and sauntered around the universe. Vishnu, realising that Shiva had to be separated from Sati for the universe to survive, used his Sudarshana Chakra to separate Sati from Shiva. The chakra dissected Sati's *deh* into fifty-one parts, and her toe fell here in Udaipur. All those fifty-one sites where Sati's remains fell is worshipped as Shakti Peethas by Hindus.

"King Dhanya Manikya, the grandfather of Amar Manikya, constructed the Tripura Sundari temple at the spot where her toe fell. It is a resplendent mandir, and we must visit it one of these days, although you will not be allowed to enter because of your faith. But hush, be quiet now. The raja has entered."

A tall, sinewy and athletic Amar Manikya entered his court. Round-faced with a thin moustache, Amar was wearing a white dhoti, an ornamental kurta with an embroidered shawl hanging on his shoulder, a sword dangling from the side and a yellow crown on his head. He had become the monarch a year back, but his years in exile had taught him not to trust anyone. He always recollected how his father Deva Manikya, the erstwhile king, had gone on a killing spree, and murdered his leading army generals, because his spiritual adviser Lakshminarayana had ostensibly advised Deva that Lord Shiva had to be appeased by their sacrifice, else big misfortune awaited Tipperah.

Little did Deva realise that it was a machination undertaken by Lakshminarayana to weaken the army so that he could usurp the throne for Deva's youngest wife's son Indra. Amar sometimes thought that Lakshminarayana was romancing the young queen and Indra was their illegitimate son. Since then, Amar had been wary of anyone's advice and believed in quid pro quo.

Amar looked around the court and was pleased to see that the leading bhuiyans of Bengal were attending his raj darbar. That meant Tipperah was once again regaining prominence as the leading kingdom in Bengal, akin to his elder brother Vijaya Manikya's reign.

Tipperah had lost significant territories and troops in trying to defend itself against Sulaiman Khan Karrani.

Amar had gone to exile when Vijaya expired fifteen years ago, but he had been plotting an uprising against the ineffective monarchy of puppet king Joy, while ensconced in the thick deciduous hilly forests of Tipperah. General Ranagan Narayan, who was the real power behind the throne, was now worried about Amar's rising popularity among the tribal masses and laid a trap to assassinate him, but got killed by Amar instead.

Shortly afterwards, Amar launched an attack with his tribal warriors on Udaipur. Joy fled, but his army captured and executed him. Now, Amar was the indisputable king of Tipperah, but with leadership, came responsibilities and worries.

Amar had come to understand that water was the key to survival and prosperity in this countryside. Tipperah received plentiful rainfall during the monsoons, yet because of her hilly terrain, the water flowed down to the seas. There were many rivers, but they were mostly seasonal, and Tipperah typically suffered drought during the harsh summer months. Having stayed in exile with the hill folks for over a decade, Amar understood their struggle for existence and recognised that Tipperah needed perennial water sources for her prosperity.

Unlike his forefathers who concentrated on building temples, Amar's mission was to excavate water tanks across Tipperah. He believed religion came after livelihood, and he wanted to construct a big lake in Udaipur to provide perennial water supply to the capital and adjacent areas. He knew it would be difficult to assemble so many workers from Tipperah, and he had sent requests to all the leading Bengal chieftains to send manpower to Udaipur so that the lake could be excavated. He was ambivalent when he sent out that request, not certain whether the Bengal chieftains would agree to his request, but looking at the large assemblage, he was pleasantly surprised.

Amar greeted the court, "Namaskar. Please take your seats. I cannot tell you how delighted I am to see so many of you Bengali bhuiyans in my humble court. I truly appreciate your noble gesture in providing coolies for my lake project Amardighi. Amardighi will endeavour to provide *jal* to all residents of Udaipur and adjacent areas throughout the year. We, the people of Tipperah, will forever be indebted to you and your contributions for making Tipperah a prosperous state."

Then, turning to his general, Subuddhi Narayan, he asked, "General, could you please read out the list of zamindars who have supported us. I want to thank them individually!"

Subuddhi—which literally meant good sense—was from the Jamatia clan. In their native Kokborok language, *jama* meant tax and *jamatia* meant tax-exempt. The Jamatias were exempt from paying taxes as they were the tribe which provided soldiers to Manikya dynasty. Successive kings, in recognition of their courage, loyalty and sacrifice, had spared them from paying taxes.

Tall, slender, with an oblong face, Subuddhi had a distinct scar on his right cheek, which had formed while he was protecting his king from an attack by the spies who had come to assassinate Amar when he was in exile. A grateful Amar had appointed Subuddhi as the general when he became the emperor, deviating from the past practice of the Manikya dynasty of having Brahmins or Kshatriyas as army general.

Subuddhi drew out a sheet of paper and started reading, "We are thankful to all these rajas and zamindars who have supplied us coolies out of love and respect for our Maharaja Amar Debbarman Manikya. The formidable Chand Roy, the zamindar of Bikrampur, has supplied us seven hundred men. The renowned Basus of Bakla, Chandradwip represented by Kandarpanarayan Roy, has sent us seven hundred men. The formidable Ghazi zamindar of Bhawal in Dhaka has sent us one thousand men. We have received five hundred men from Ashtagram and another five hundred from Baniachung, Sylhet. We have got one thousand men from the eminent Rana of Bhawal and one thousand men have been supplied by our neighbour, the esteemed Isa Khan of Sarail. We have got one thousand men from the illustrious Balaram Sur of Bhulua, Noakhali!"

"We have thus secured 6,400 coolies from these generous rulers and our excavation work is going on at full speed. We expect to complete the water tank in another two weeks, but we would be pleased to take all you dignitaries to the site so that you can appreciate what your people have created. We are thankful to each of you for providing us these industrious and clever men. And now, our maharaja would like to individually felicitate each of you."

Amar arose from his chair and announced,

"Please accept this *lasingphee* as a gesture of appreciation for your valuable contribution. It is woven by the tribals on the looms. I cannot thank you enough and will always be obliged to each one of you."

Amar approached each of the bhuiyans individually and wrapped the checked cotton shawl around their shoulders.

He turned to Subuddhi and asked, "General, I presume all the zamindars to whom we sent the request for assistance contributed to this campaign."

Subuddhi announced, "Maharaja, Fateh Khan, the raja of Tarap from Sylhet refused to send any men!"

"Surely, he must have sent some words as to why he could not participate in my dream project."

Subuddhi lowered his voice and replied, "Maharaja, he refused to send any *dut*, saying we were a *rajya* under decline. He said since we could not withstand the Karranis, he prefers to pay his obeisance to Akbar instead!"

This was a slap on Amar's face, especially in front of all these dignitaries. He glared at Subuddhi.

"We need to send our troops and give a fitting reply to Fateh Khan. We cannot allow adversaries to prevail on us, especially at our borders. This will foment dissent and it is not healthy for our kingdom. You will accompany my *putra* Rajdhar who will lead this expedition, and I want Fateh to be imprisoned and brought to me."

He looked around the court. "Does anyone want to speak up?"

Isa instantly stood up and said, "Maharaja, you rule a hilly state where you are not accustomed to naval warfare. Summer is ending. Soon, the entire eastern Bengal, including Sylhet, will be inundated. Your army will be stranded on land, surrounded by pani, and the crafty Fateh Khan will use the advantage of the seasonal rivers to harass your army and inflict massive casualties. I believe your army should have naval backup so that if Fateh Khan tries to flee in shuluks, they can be contained in the rivers."

Amar was impressed.

He said, "That is an excellent suggestion. But we do not have a navy. What do you suggest we do?"

"Make me the senapati of your naval army. I will supply the men and the boats."

"I, Maharaja Amar Debbarman Manikya, hereby appoint Isa Khan as the commander of Tipperah's naval troop. May you prevail in your battles!"

13

The Mughal Army Retreats

AD 1578

ISA MARCHED ON HIS HORSE at the head of his army, along with his general Karimullah, to meet the Mughal army head on in Tangail. Masood now rechristened Karimullah was the general of Isa's army. He was a towering figure, muscular and black, with a shaved head, and invoked fear in the opposition by his mere presence.

Isa turned to Karimullah and said, "Strange is the will of Allah! I was all prepared, ready to set out for *jang* against Tarap with Yuvaraj Rajdhar when your messenger came and informed me that the Delhi Sultanate was attacking Sarail. A day late and the messenger would have missed me."

Khan Jahan, the nephew of Akbar's mentor Bairam Khan, the reigning subahdar of Bengal, the person responsible for slaughtering the Karrani dynasty, was now headed towards Sarail to vanquish Isa. An emissary had been sent in advance to Sarail, with the demand for paying a *khajna* of one lakh taka, including past dues, or else the land would be captured by the subahdar. On receiving the notice of the tax demand, Karimullah—the resident caretaker of Sarail in the absence of Isa—had immediately summoned an envoy and said, "*Jaldi jao* to Tipperah and warn Isa of the impending attack".

Unknown to Isa, the Roys of Jessore—Bhikam and Basanta—had grown tired of hiding in the forests and had surrendered to Khan Jahan. In exchange of the tax records and a part of the wealth they had looted from Tanda, their zamindari at Jessore was restored.

Khan Jahan waited for the spring harvest to record the revenue inflows and then commenced his journey to Sarail to crush the upstart Isa. He was confident that vanquishing one bhuiyan would mean everyone else would fall in line in paying the tax.

Karimullah said, "Masnad-i-Ala, you could have very well stayed away and let the Mughals plunder Sarail. After all, you have no family here and nothing to lose should Sarail be destroyed. You could have well continued your journey to Tarap with your soldiers and gained the favour of the Tipperah maharaja. But I am grateful that you returned, and that too with such a large army. How could you muster such a great army in so short a time? I am confident victory will be upon us!"

Isa loved the way Karimullah addressed him as "Masnad-i-Ala", literally meaning the highest power.

"Never again say I have no *khandan* here. You are my family; the people here are my family. As a ruler, it is my *farz* to protect my kingdom. I will always be there to lead my army to warfare whenever the situation demands, although my strategy might vary. Today, I am marching to meet the Mughals because I am comforted by the strength of my *fauj*, but if I had even an iota of doubt that I would be defeated, I would have employed guerrilla tactics and played a cat and mouse game with the Mughals."

Karimullah nodded silently.

"When I heard that the Mughals were approaching us, I knew I needed to do something quick to withstand the forces of the sultanate. Apart from you and your brethren who arrived from Qazvin, my soldiers here have all been trained by me. I am unsure whether they can defend themselves successfully against the Mughal onslaught. You know how I have been endeavouring to develop alliances with other bhuiyans, but I have only been successful in developing ties with the stronger bhuiyans of Chandradwip and Sripur. I could have asked them for *madad*, but we did not have the time to marshal their troops from the south and join us in the battle.

"The smaller zamindars do not know where their allegiance lies and keep debating whether they should become independent or pay taxes to the Bengal Sultanate. Meanwhile, I am looked down by both Hindu and Muslim gentry. Hindus avoid me since I am a Muslim whereas Muslims abhor me as I have Hindu blood. You remember how Musa's marriage proposal with the princess of Tazpur was rejected?"

Under Fatima's constant cajoling, Isa felt that the nubile Princess Amira would be a suitable match for Musa.

However, Omar Khan, her father turned down the proposal and admonished the emissary, "Your Isa is a kafir. He has Hindu *khoon* and is guided by Hindu tastes. How dare you propose his son's name as my beti's suitor!"

"Yes, I was astonished the way Omar Khan, who lords over a much smaller region than Sarail, rejected your proposal. I am new here, but I understand the situation. The original Mussalmans from Persia, the Ashrafs, look down upon the converts, the Ajlafs. I feel it strange and see this as an ignorance of the Allah's sermons, for Shah Tahmasp did not differentiate between the originals and the converts. To him, all Mussalmans were equal. The ignorance of the Muslims here is not a reflection of their innocence but a reflection of their gullibility!"

Isa smiled.

"You have the gift of the gab, Karimullah. I am sure you must have learnt well under the shah and the shehzadi. And now, may you be successful in battle too. A name like yours should create fear among enemies. Now I understand why Rajib rechristened himself Kalapahad."

"Masnad-i-Ala, you have still not answered my question!"

"You are one adamant general, Karimullah. In the past, I had dreamt of unifying the zamindars of eastern Bengal, but the fiasco with Omar Khan reminded me that one cannot trust the Ashraf Muslims. That day, I realised that Chand Ghazi and Fazl Ghazi only behave as my friends—I do not think they truly consider me their *dost*. The Ashrafs also have their feet in two boats, unsure of whether to challenge the Mughals or accept their suzerainty. The support of the Ajlafs is no consolation for me in my fight against the Mughals as they are mainly peasants or minor officials, and do not enjoy the landownership that could make them formidable allies.

"I need to turn to the Hindus, eager as they are to protect their land from all the various invaders, and my appeal as a Bengali for an independent Bengal transcends religion and makes me acceptable to them, provided I can win their trust. Hence, I went to Tipperah to obtain the confidence of the maharaja, fully aware that his approval would help me gain the trust of the fence-sitters.

"I was prepared to ride out in battle, supporting the *rajkumar*, when your message arrived. I, immediately, took it to the maharaja. He was concerned but offered no support. I knew I had to do something impactful and discussed with the Afghans employed in his troop. They advised me that Queen Amaravati Devi was the key to Maharaja Amar Manikya's heart and to gain his favour, I required her approval.

"Thus, I immediately wrote a letter to the queen, stating that I looked forward to leading the navy while her son Rajdhar led the campaign to vanquish Fateh Khan of Sylhet, but in the meantime, I had to leave for Sarail on short notice as the Mughals were invading my province, and I hoped to return soon to join the campaign against Sylhet. I requested her to accept me as her beta."

"That was a brilliant strategy. What did the queen do? And that still does not explain how you ended up with an additional fifty thousand soldiers!"

Isa laughed.

"Karimullah, you are trying to peel an onion layer by layer. That will take you an eternity to arrive at the full story.

Suffice it to say that Amaravati Debi was enthralled by my audacity to stand up to the Mughals. She said she wished she had more sons like me, and that protecting one's kingdom was the principal dharma of a king. She admonished the maharaja for not supporting me in my mission, and said that if Sarail fell, Tippcrah could be the next target of the Mughals. She said that if I succeeded in withstanding the Mughals, Tipperah could become the leading independent kingdom in the eastern region, supported by the Bengali bhuiyans.

"That is how the maharaja volunteered to divert all his troops, including elephants, to support my expedition. He even requested the other bhuiyans to send their coolies who had been working on the now-completed Amardighi mission to accompany me. Amar Manikya believes we should approach the Mughals with such a huge army that the sultanate is overwhelmed and refuses to campaign in the east over the next few decades."

Karimullah marvelled at Amar Manikya's foresight.

"Did the queen send any token accepting you as her son?"

Isa's face reddened.

"She gave me the ultimate gift any son can think of. On the day of my departure from Udaipur, she called me to the royal chambers. She said that she was fortunate in having me as her son. She said that she may not have given birth to me, but the greatest satisfaction of a mother was not giving birth but providing milk to her child for nourishment."

Isa paused, looking a little embarrassed and then continued, "It appears Amaravati Devi woke up in the morning, washed her breasts with milk and rose water, which she collected in a silver bowl and offered me to drink it. She apologised that her breast milk had dried up and she was unable to offer me her milk, but as per the scriptures, this was an acceptable means of acknowledging a person as a child.

"I was amazed by the queen's gesture and was dumbfounded how to express my gratitude! I touched her feet and thanked her for her generosity and then slowly sipped the milk. Now, I can claim to be part of the Chandravansha dynasty, though my father-in-law will not be pleased about it."

Karimullah laughed out aloud.

"You are indeed treading a tightrope!"

As they chatted, the mighty Sarail–Tipperah army, with its fifty-five thousand soldiers, cavalry, elephants and cannons trudged through the sun-parched fields of Bengal. When Isa had started from Sarail, his spies had informed him that the enemy, with over five thousand soldiers, was crossing the Jamuna River, and now they returned to inform him that Khan Jahan had camped on the opposite side of the Louhajang River.

As Isa's army approached the river, he shouted, "*Sipahis*, spread out. I want the Mughal army to see us from afar. I want the drums to be beaten loudly and in unison so that the reverberations send shivers down the spine of the so-called Mughals."

It was around dusk that Isa announced his arrival to the Mughals. As they camped on the opposite bank of the Louhajang River, ready to battle the Mughals the next dawn, Khan Jahan came out to inspect the opposition. Throughout his long illustrious career as a general in Akbar's army, he had never been so hopelessly outnumbered as he was now. He could see the enemy matched him in cannons, horses and elephants, but it was the sheer size of their army that bewildered him. Khan Jahan was most impressed looking at the general of his enemy's army—the man was huge and even stronger than Kalapahad. As Khan Jahan retreated to his tent, he pondered about his strategy to combat Isa Khan.

Karimullah woke up early the next day. The last few months had been a whirlwind for him, packed with a lifetime's experience. The departure from Qazvin, the arduous trek to Sarail, the chance to eke out a new life—not as a slave but as a free citizen—in a distant land, all stood out. However, his proudest moment—one which he would recall to Isa's children later in life—was waking up on the morning of his first war as an army general and seeing no signs of the enemy.

Khan Jahan had realised that it would be perilous to meet the enemy in an open war and had hastily retreated in the midst of the night, hoping that Isa would chase them so that they could be caught in ambush.

Karimullah rushed to Isa's tent and enquired, "Masnad-i-Ala, should we chase the Mughals?"

"We first need to consolidate our territories here before we think of chasing them. The Mughals will not attack in the monsoon, but they will be back next year. Next time, they will attack by stealth. For the time being, it is far more important to subdue Sylhet for a stable Bengal."

14

A Vision in White

It was the Bengali New Year, the fourteenth day of April 1583, the day to celebrate the harvest. All the leading bhuiyans and zamindars had assembled in Sripur to mark the happy occasion on the invitation of Kedar Roy. Various shuluks, *shampans* and bajras from all over the region had descended on the ghat of Sripur and it was to be a night of merriment. Every landowner worth his salt was attending because behind the gaiety and exuberance lay their anxiety about the future of Bengal.

The key question everyone was grappling with was whether to pay taxes to the Mughals or revolt and stop paying taxes. The landowners needed to maintain a force to protect the crops and the land, employ people for revenue collection and have an administrative set-up for record keeping, which had to be financed from the tax collections. It was indeed a catch-22 situation.

The landlords knew that increasing taxes would cripple the farmers while lowering taxes would lead to their financial ruin. Everyone was looking for guidance from Isa—his fame had spread far and wide after his triumph against the Mughals in Tangail, his successful attack on Sylhet and the patronage that he enjoyed of the Tipperah royal family.

Raja Lakshman Manikya, who claimed his descendance from Adisura and ruled Bhuluya in southern Noakhali, approached Isa, "*Shubho Noboborsho,* Isa babu. I am truly impressed by your achievements in the past few years. I marvel at your acumen and political insight. However, I was flummoxed when you shifted your capital to Sonargaon, closer to the leading chieftains of Sripur and Chandradwip, when you could have been safely ensconced in Sarail. My province is sandwiched between Tipperah and Chandradwip, and I am forever worried about attacks on my frontiers from these rival provinces.

"Look at me! I have sworn my allegiance to the Tipperah royal family and pay them an annual protection money so that they defend Bhuluya from any advances from Chandradwip. I have even assumed their title, forsaking the surname of my illustrious forefathers!"

Isa indeed had shifted his residence to Sonargaon earlier in the year 1583 after the conquest of Sylhet. He had been impressed by the wealth of Sylhet.

Isa had often heard but now understood that eastern Bengal was the granary of the subcontinent. His experience in Sarail wherein he had quickly converted a forested area into a prosperous region bore testimony to the same. He contemplated, *If this riverine countryside could protect its crops and its income, it could finance and withstand any onslaught by the opposition.*

"Shubho Noboborsho to you too. It seems paradoxical that while the great king Shashanka of Gaur introduced the Bengali calendar almost a millennium ago, it was my maternal great-grandfather who introduced the celebration of the Bengali new year. It is my privilege to be with my fellow Bengalis today."

"Yes, Allaudin Hussain Shah was a visionary!"

Isa smiled in acknowledgement.

"I have endeavoured to make Sarail prosperous. Yet, I realise that its flat terrain makes it an easy target for enemies. I had the misfortune of seeing my father decapitated in battle in Sarail against the Karranis because that area offered no military fortification. Thus, I shifted my family to Sonargaon on the fall of the Karrani dynasty so that my progeny could be protected. And on vanquishing the Mughals, when I realised I had the chance of shifting to the well-fortified town of Sonargaon, I did just that.

"What pains me is that we treat our fellow neighbours as enemies, while we do not address our main enemies—our invaders. Genghis Khan once said that one could bend one arrow but not bend ten arrows tied together. In our unity lies our strength and our destiny to create a new Bengal."

An aged, religious-looking person was listening to their conversation and now approached Isa and Lakshman.

Addressing Isa, he said, "If I am not mistaken, you are the putra of Kalidas and the nephew of Ramdas. It seems just yesterday that your uncle came to seek help to trace you. May Goddess Tara bless you!"

Isa, genuflected and said, "*Pronam*, Chand babu. Our family will always be indebted to you. I have heard from my uncle how you introduced him to Sridhara babu which enabled him to track me down to Turan."

Chand smiled.

"Shukriya, Isa. I am aware of all the upheavals you faced, and I am pleased to see you have risen above all those challenges to establish yourself as a successful bhuiyan. I hear stories about the prosperity of your peasants, and how they proclaim you have brought back Ram Rajya. I truly salute you!"

"Chand babu, I am just doing my duty as a ruler."

Kedar Roy came to join them, accompanied by Kandarpanarayan and another gentleman. Isa hugged Kedar and Kandarpanarayan.

"It is good to see you have met my elder brother Chand. Let me introduce you to Pratapaditya, the son of Sridhara. You remember we met at his *shaadi*!"

Isa nodded.

"It is my privilege to meet you, Pratapaditya. We were just reminiscing about your baba and his role in tracking me down."

But even as he said that, Isa could see a momentary rage in Pratapaditya's eyes. A confused Isa thought, *Is he angry with his father or me*? He looked around. *Did no one else notice the fury in Pratapaditya's eyes*?

Chand said, "Pratap, you are the spitting image of your baba although your moustache is more prominent! May his soul rest in peace."

Pratapaditya grimaced.

He looked at Isa and said, "Masnad-i-Ala, I was looking forward to meeting you. Your victories speak about you. I seek your *mashorah* on how we structure our stratagem against the Mughals. Do we pay taxes to them? Have you? In case we stop paying taxes to them, the Mughals will come to loot us. Not every time can we have an army of over fifty thousand soldiers with us."

Isa's eyes sparkled as Pratapaditya made his observations. Isa thought, *Finally, someone has raised the issue. I have come to the ceremony only to debate on precisely these aspects and understand whether the various zamindars are interested in putting up a unified front.*

"Excellent thoughts, Pratap babu", and then looking at all the other people in the room, he continued, "*Dosto,* Pratap babu here from the house of Jessore asked me whether I have stopped paying taxes to the Mughals, and in that case, how do I plan to resist the Mughals.

"Well, truth be told, I have not been paying taxes to the Mughals for a few years now, due to which I have been able to raise a reasonable army, strengthen the forts around the Meghna and Shitalakshya rivers, and ensure my people are well-fed. If the Mughals take one-third or half of our crops as revenue, how will our people and fauj survive? And even if they survive, how do we sustain ourselves?

"Respected guests, I do not know how many of you know about my past travails. I stayed as a slave for over a decade in distant Turan. It was a tough life, and I feel blessed to be born in Bengal. I have travelled across northern India, and I have never encountered such fertile lands that we have here. Kandahar, which we call Gandhara here, is a rocky terrain, and so is Turan. It is so difficult to grow crops there, and here we do not even need to sow rice seeds. Our land and climate are so blessed that we can grow rice thrice a year. Because the west of Hindustan is so barren, the Turks, Mongols and Afghans attack Delhi to plunder her wealth, a *daulat* that is our largesse to them.

"When I was a soldier in the Suri army, I gathered that Sher Shah enjoyed the taxes of Bengal for around four to five years to develop his war chest, and then marched against Humayun to defeat him. But we do not need to attack the Mughals. Let us enjoy our *zamin* and its gifts and let the Mughals come and attack us!"

Isa paused and looked around the room. Everyone was listening to him with rapt attention.

"The flipside of such prosperity is that we have become lazy and self-contented. Imagine, in which other region could Bakhtiyar Khilji walk in with eighteen horsemen and usurp the throne, while our king Lakshmana Sena fled to this place where we are now standing!"

Glancing at Chand and Kedar Roy, Isa continued, "The Sripur Roys have identified the perfect location to protect themselves against invaders. For here, in the confluence of the mighty Padma, Dhaleshwari and Meghna, lies a province which is virtually impregnable by the invaders for most part of the year. We need to develop such unsurmountable locations for each of us. Some of you may know that I have shifted my base from Sarail to Sonargaon because it offers me the same strategic locational advantage that Sripur enjoys. Or for that matter, Chandradwip. The greatest advantage we enjoy is that this territory is virtually inaccessible for almost six months from the advent of the monsoon which means we need to concentrate on *jang* for only six months in a year.

"Warfare has evolved. I have taught my son swordsmanship, but I realise the art of battle has now gravitated towards mortar and gunpowder. Our archery is also no longer our strength. Protected by these rivers, we know that elephants cannot charge at our walls, while the cannons from our forts can decimate the *dushman* even before they have crossed the rivers. Look at Sripur, the Roys have placed cannons at strategic locations across their kingdoms to combat the enemies. Thus, we do not need to maintain armies of thirty or fifty thousand strength. An army of five thousand soldiers can defend our territories well. By joining hands with Kedar babu and Kandarpanarayan babu, we will ensure we protect each other's back and rise together to fight invasions."

A murmur of discontent rang through the room. Isa realised he had only talked about his issues, and not addressed the concerns of the people gathered there.

"Gentleman, you all need to reflect on your own strategy. Taharpur, Dinajpur, Rajshahi and Natore zamindars—you need to assess whether you can protect yourselves from Mughal attacks since you are too far from us, and we cannot immediately support you in times of your need. Raja Lakshman Manikya, I suggest you continue to pay your taxes to the Tipperah maharaja because if you stop doing so, their army could attack you.

"Raja Mukundaram of Bhushna, your area in Faridpur is vulnerable to *humla* from the Mughals again. Reconsider your tactics—maybe, you can pay reduced taxes to be on the good books of the Mughals."

And then looking at the Ghazis, he said, "The same applies to you, Chand babu and Fazl babu. But it is also important that we educate the villagers so that they can resort to drumbeats whenever there is enemy movement in their areas, and others to join in sounding the drum whenever they hear a drum beat from an adjacent village.

"The first village which plays the *dhol* should make one beat every minute, the next village which relays the sounds from the first village must make two beats after every two minutes, the next village three beats after every three minutes, so that we also know how far away the enemy is. Sound travels faster than the enemy and this will ensure we are prepared for any invasion to defend the *azadi* of Bengal and let only her people enjoy her resources."

Everyone gave Isa a standing ovation. The drinks started flowing while fish chops, mutton cutlets and *kachim* fries were devoured, and everyone chatted on the future of Bengal, including how to build her defences, how to protect her crops, whether the Portuguese should be introduced in their army, what boats to include to excel in naval warfare and women of which province to be had in bed for the best entertainment.

When the dawn was nearing, a sozzled Isa got up and addressed the gathering, "*Pahela prahar sab koi jaage, dusrah prahar bhogi, teesra prahar taskar jaage, choutha prahar yogi* (Everyone is awake during the first quarter of the night; the second quarter is for enjoying sensual and earthly pleasures; thieves remain awake during the third and ascetics arise in the fourth.). Today, we are fulfilling all the four roles by staying awake through the *raat*. But while the Mughals might say we are plundering from them, tomorrow's Bengal will remember us as crusaders for a new Bengal."

As Isa took everyone's leave, Chand Roy asked Sanatan to escort Isa to the ghat. While they trudged towards his *kosha*, Isa noticed a petite, young lady drying her long wet hair with a *gamchha* on Raj Badi's rooftop. Noticing her white sari, Isa understood she was a widow. Through the wet and translucent sari, Isa could make out the outline of her voluptuous breasts. Isa was transfixed. *She looks so much like Pari,* Isa couldn't help thinking.

The lady sensed someone staring at her and looked straight at Isa. Their eyes met. Isa felt he was staring into the deep, dark eyes of his Pari. The alluring woman got embarrassed and darted towards the stairs. Isa's face almost turned crimson as he suddenly realised Sanatan's presence. *I hope he has not noticed my indiscretion.*

The wily Sanatan did not miss anything. In silence, they walked towards the jetty.

As Isa was about to board his boat, he heard someone calling out, "Isa babu! Isa babu!" Isa looked back in surprise. Masum Khan—the zamindar of Dinajpur—was rushing towards him. He wore a worried expression on his face.

"Isa babu, my emissary has just arrived saying that the Mughals are invading Dinajpur!"

Isa looked at Masum and calmly said, "Ask your army to move to Sarail while you follow me to my kosha!"

15

Shatranj ke Khiladi

ONCE ISA AND MASUM SETTLED inside the kosha, Isa said, "Masum Khan, It was a pleasure meeting you at Raj Badi. Although it was our first meeting, I have heard about your revolt against the subahdar of Bengal. Truth be told, I am not sure where your priorities lie! Aren't you with the enemy's camp?"

Masum shook his head vehemently and chuckled.

"Is that why you have invited me to your *jahaz*? *Subhanallah*, I am impressed. I can see you want to keep your friends close but your enemies closer. I am sure the few years you spent in the Safavid court must have helped you in developing your military acumen."

Isa smiled.

"Why, you think we Bengalis are incapable of such strategy and ingenuity?"

"Sorry, do not take me otherwise. I hail from Khorasan, and I am a proud Turbat-i Sayyid, hence my partiality!"

Isa relaxed.

"What a small world! We must exchange notes. We have all the time now. I believe people from your region are men of honour although I do not understand the Mughals. After we defeated them five summers ago, I have been waiting for the Mughals to regroup and attack us, as is expected from descendants of the two of the greatest conquerors in history—Genghis Khan and Timur. You will not believe the stories I have heard of Genghis and Timur while in Qazvin, and I must say, while the brutality and the barbarism of the Mongols nauseate me, their principles inspire me."

Masum nodded.

"Yes, the Mongols, when they attacked, spared none and left behind scorched villages and mutilated bodies. Genghis Khan's greatest happiness was to vanquish his enemies, chase them, rob them of their wealth, and rape their wives and daughters.

"The chronicler Ibn al-Athir said of the Mongols, 'They killed women, men, children, ripped open the bodies of the pregnant and slaughtered the unborn.' But why look west for instances of barbarism when we have seen how the Mughals massacred the Karrani dynasty even after they surrendered at the Battle of Rajmahal."

Isa sighed in agreement.

"Right from the time we defeated Khan Jahan, I have been expecting a Mughal attack and have stationed spies at Tanda. Khan Jahan could not accept the ignominy of running away from the battlefield on facing a local upstart like me, and I am told, depression and despondency led to his untimely death. The governor of Bihar, Muzaffar Khan Turbati was given the additional charge of Bengal."

Isa paused and asked, "Masum bhai, I know you were a jagirdar in Bihar when Muzaffar Khan Turbati got the additional governorship of Bengal, and I knew Akbar's decree to Muzaffar was to demolish rebel chieftains like me, yet you challenged him! Why did you oppose Turbati?"

Masum reflected for a while, and then responded, "Mian, I am the foster-brother of Mirza Muhammad Hakim, the brother of Akbar. When Hakim ruled Kandahar, I was his right-hand man; but when it was attacked in 1566, Hakim fled. I succeded in defending Kabul and became its governor.

"Sometime later, I had a conflict with Hakim's brother-in-law and relinquished my governorship and sought allegiance with Akbar who gave me the jagirdar in Patna, and that is how I came to Hindustan!

"However, Muzaffar Khan Turbati was drunk in power. He openly claimed that Akbar was the emperor of Hindustan because of him. He identified a few large jagirdars, including myself, and redistributed our lands to send us a message that he was the lord. But when he ordered that land revenues be placed under the direct control of the sultanate instead of at the disposal of the *mansabdar*s, we revolted, and praise be to Allah, Akbar sided with us!"

Isa interrupted Masum as a bearer brought in food *luchi*, *chholar dal* and *daaber jol*.

"Please, help yourself to some *nashta*. After yesterday's sumptuous *dawat*, I thought we should have something light. But this is interesting. I was not aware that you are a foster-brother of Hakim's. It must have been interesting times when Akbar's foster-brother Mirza Aziz became governor of Bengal and Bihar. Since both you and Aziz are foster-brothers of Humayun's sons, are you both also related?"

Masum laughed.

"Hakim is the son of Mah Chuchak Begum. Remind me one day to tell you about Mah Chuchak and her exploits. She was an extraordinary lady who ruled Kabul independently and even led her army to defeat Munim Khan—the same Munim Khan who later defeated Daud and became governor of Bengal. But I am digressing. Mirza is the son of Akbar's wet nurse. I am the son of Hakim's wet nurse. But you were asking me about Mirza's rule as governor of Bengal."

"Yes," said Isa. "Why have the Mughals not attacked us all this while?"

"Maybe it is the heat and the humidity. Akbar had sent Mirza so that he would be acceptable to us and had instructed him to ensure revenue maximisation. Mirza just believed in epicureanism and indulged in various pleasure, placating the various rebel chiefs by granting bigger zamindaris. Thus, he granted me the zamindars of Dinajpur. But Mirza did not follow up on the revenues."

Sipping the daaber jol, Masum continued, "You may be knowing that Akbar's army has been busy campaigning in Mewar for the past few years, trying to demolish the resistance of Maharana Pratap. The Mughals captured Mewar in the Battle of Haldighati around seven years back but could not capture Maharana Pratap or his family members. Maharana Pratap has adopted the guerrilla tactic against the Mughals, which is an irritant to Akbar and a blow to his ego. Military campaigns require funds, but

Mirza's ineffective administration had resulted in dwindling revenues in the emperor's coffers.

"Akbar realised that vanquishing Maharana Pratap was a matter of prestige but having a strong and ruthless administrator in Bengal was imperative for sustaining military adventures. Akbar therefore withdrew his successful commander Shahbaz Khan from the Mewar campaign and appointed him subahdar of Bengal. One of the key qualities of Shahbaz, apart from being a fearless soldier, is that he is a devout Muslim and is not swayed by worldly pleasures."

"I am aware of Shahbaz Khan's appointment, and I have been fearing an imminent attack on Sonargaon, which is why I spoke last night of the need for all of us to get united against the Mughals, but what I fail to understand is why they are attacking Dinajpur."

Isa stopped, thought for a minute and then asked Masum, "Have you been paying your taxes to the Mughals?"

Masum sheepishly grinned.

"I haven't paid any khajna ever since I became the zamindar of Dinajpur."

Isa was shocked.

"Masum mian, you must be aware that Dinajpur is very prosperous. Not paying taxes is a sign of rebellion and your territory lies close to Tanda. How could you peril your *qaum* and your family through such heedless action?"

Then, noticing the downcast Masum, Isa consoled him, "Do not worry, you will be safe with me."

They had finished their breakfast. Isa invited Masum to climb up to the deck.

"We call this boat a kosha because it is a *kosh* long. The boat can accommodate a thousand rowers and it flies when everyone rows."

Masum could see the kosha speeding across the Meghna, while the boatswain shouted to the fisherfolks, "Stay away from the bow waves!"

"We are now speeding up the Meghna and you can see Sonargaon on the left, but our strategy will be to draw the enemy to the other side of Sonargaon on the Shitalakshya River. There, I will fire cannons and arrows from my forts on the invaders. But I want to catch the enemy unawares, and hence I asked your troops to move to Sarail. The Bhati region will soon be under water when the monsoon commences, and I hope the Mughals get stranded there. However, if they have come prepared for naval warfare, I will draw them to the forts and then pulverise them."

Masum chuckled.

"Isa mian, this is the difference between an administrative landlord and a warrior chieftain. You think about all the possible inevitabilities, and you accordingly plan your moves in advance, while we dwell from one season to the next, taking things as they come. You remind me of a *shatranj* player, well in control of your chess board!"

It was the month of summer when the air was still, and while the ship was moving upstream, it made good progress. As the kosha approached Sarail, Isa was pleased to notice that neither Masum's troops nor the Mughal invaders had arrived. He straightaway went to the Portuguese residential area, and called upon their prominent leaders, Gonsalves and Carvalho. Isa had enlisted the support of these two men to develop his navy and they had stayed back in Sarail subsequently.

Isa appraised them of the developing situation.

"The Mughals have invaded Dinajpur, and I have advised the army there to come and meet me here at Sarail. As soon as they arrive, I will board them on my kosha, wait for the arrival of the Mughal army and then set sail for Sonargaon. Ask your men to draw the trench bridges and retreat behind the forests, though I would request the two of you to join me on the kosha. Your marksmanship will be extremely valuable to us as we fight these Mughals!"

The next day, anchored on the Meghna, Isa, Masum, Gonsalves and Carvalho chatted about the various zamindars and their idiosyncrasies, discussed the various vegetables and fruits, like batata, *bilayati begoon*, *bhindi*, *gobhi* and *peyara*, which the Portuguese had introduced.

"We know what the ubiquitous aloo did to my father and how it changed his life. But why just vegetables. The luchi has become so much fluffier and tastier ever since the Portuguese introduced refined flour. Truly, you people know that the way to a man's heart is through the stomach!"

And as they laughed, gossiped and entertained each other, while complaining about the summer heat and humidity, a guard came running and said, "Saheb, the army is in sight."

Isa and Masum went up to the deck to inspect and looking at the nearly one thousand soldiers on horseback and foot, with no cannons or elephants, concluded it was the Dinajpuri soldiers.

Masum was despondent.

"This is only a fraction of my army. What happened to the rest? Are they decimated?"

Isa consoled him.

"Maybe the army dispersed to protect themselves. We will find out soon."

The senapati, on arrival, confirmed Isa's suspicion.

"You should have seen the Mughal army. The fury of the Mughals forced our army to separate and move in different directions, and a large chunk crossed the Jamuna and made way to Assam, while the fleet-footed soldiers and the cavalry rode to Sarail. Dinajpur had been scorched by the Mughals, but everyone had escaped based on your timely advice through the emissary. *Huzoor*, the Mughals are approaching with a vengeance."

It was nearing dusk and Isa urged the soldiers to board the kosha.

As the troops boarded the kosha, Isa noticed the dust in the horizon. He asked the men, "Hurry. The enemies are fast approaching. We need to set sail before they are here."

Isa commanded the captain to start the kosha when the Mughal army became visible. "That way, the Mughals will chase us, rather than ravage Sarail."

As evening descended, the ship silently sailed down the Meghna, but as they neared the confluence of the Meghna, Dhaleshwari and Padma at Sripur, Isa instructed the captain to anchor for the night.

Masum enquired, "Why are you stopping in the middle of this wilderness amidst this vast expanse of water?"

"I want the Mughals to follow us. I presume they will rest tonight and start tomorrow. If the Mughals start tomorrow morning and follow us on boats, I expect them to arrive the day after. We have positioned ourselves here so that they do not lose our trail, and we can lure them into the Shitalakshya River through the Dhaleshwari. However, in case a part of their army comes by land, I do not want us to be sitting ducks. Hence, we have anchored in the middle of this vast expanse of water where *golis* fired from the land will not impact us."

"*Wah*!"

"Tomorrow, you and your men can relax. I propose to pay a courtesy call to Chand Roy and Kedar Roy in the morning."

Next day, before dawn, Isa boarded a dinghy and came to Sripur. As he alighted, Sanatan came running to meet him.

"It is such a privilege to be graced by your presence again."

As they walked towards the Raj Badi, Isa's eyes scanned the rooftop. Sure enough, the bewitching lady in white was there. She was even more beautiful than Pari. It was clearly love renewed at first sight for Isa.

Who is she? Isa pondered as he scratched his chin.

The lady also noticed him and stepped behind a pillar though Isa could make out she was peeping at him.

He could not bear the suspense any more. Isa turned to Sanatan and asked, "Who is the lady in white on the terrace?"

Without even battling an eyelid, Sanatan replied, "She is Sona didi, Chand Roy's only daughter. Sadly, she is a widow."

Isa nodded.

Hmm, it seemed so ...

"You seem to have a strong fascination for her, Isa babu."

Running his bony fingers through his slick hair, Sanatan added, "I can bring her to you if you desire."

Isa was startled to hear this from Chand Roy's trusted secretary. He reflected, *With trusted officials like this, even friends could not save Sripur from her enemies*!

16

The Chase

Isa woke up with a start.

He scratched himself thinking aloud, *Was that a dream? It was so weird ...*

> He was lying naked with Pari at Kolah Farangi, wrapped in each other's embrace, discussing about their future, when suddenly Pari screamed, "The palace is on fire!"
>
> As the flames engulfed the mansion, both realised it was pointless moving downstairs. They hurriedly dressed and ran to the terrace, and saw the palace surrounded by Mughals, screaming for their blood. As they searched for an escape route, Pari's silk gown caught fire. The fire rapidly spread and Pari was ablaze.
>
> Clutching onto Isa's wrist, Pari jumped into the Ganga. But such was the fury of the fire that the water evaporated, and the lovers sank into an abyss of darkness.

Suddenly, Isa got distracted by a loud knocking sound. He gingerly made his way to the source of the sound in pitch darkness and found himself against a door. As he pushed it with all his strength, the door broke open, and the chamber was flooded with light. Pari had now vanished, and Sona was now next to him, with cobras and pythons slithering all around. It appeared the snakes were fighting a battle of annihilation, but seeing Isa and Sona, they stopped their fight to attack the two.

Sona was terrified, but Isa comforted her, "Don't be scared. I am an expert swordsman, and I will slaughter these serpents." But the snakes were too many in number, appeared from every direction—including the ceiling—and one python wrapped itself around Isa's sword such that Isa could not manoeuvre it any more. Meanwhile, the knocking had now transformed into banging, and Isa was trembling, wondering about further adversities.

Out of the blue, Isa heard Karimullah's booming voice, "Masnad-i-Ala, open the door!"

"Wait!"

Isa took in the darkness of the room, and looked out of the window. The faint golden bloom on the horizon reminded him that it would be morning soon. He slowly sprang from his bed and quickly opened the door.

"Sardar, the Mughals are attacking!"

As Isa ran out on the deck, he noticed that the kosha had started moving. He asked Karimullah, "Who ordered the ship to start?"

"Sardar, I had to order the captain to start it for our safety."

Isa looked out, and saw the river was teeming with fishing boats, and it was evident that the Mughals wanted to catch Isa and his men unawares. Isa rubbed his chin as he pondered, *The Mughals must have journeyed through the night to launch a surprise attack on us in the midst of darkness. I am glad I asked Karimullah and a few trusted soldiers to join me in the kosha.*

"Shukriya, Karimullah. I am sure most people would have failed to notice the boats in the darkness until it was too late, and we were surrounded. These fishing boats hardly make any noise, and since they are almost at level with the *dariya*, it is difficult to spot them from the kosha."

Karimullah grinned.

"I was only doing my job, Masnad-i-Ala."

Indeed, Karimullah had spotted the boats early. The Mughals wanted to approach the kosha silently and knew that by the time they were spotted, they would be close to the ship. It would take time for the crew to start the boat, and those precious minutes would give the advantage to the Mughals to ram their boats against the starboard. The Mughals were sure the kosha would topple under the impact of the poundings, but they had not anticipated being spotted the moment they arrived at the horizon. Karimullah had first run down to wake up the captain and the crew, ordered them to start the ship immediately, instructed the Dinajpuri archers to hasten to the deck, went back to check the progress of the Mughals and only then had gone to awaken Isa.

The nearest boats were only around a hundred feet away and Isa knew that they had started not a moment too soon. He saw the archers from both sides taking aim. Isa heaved a sigh and smiled to himself, *My army has the advantage of attacking from a height.* As arrows flew, he saw several Mughal soldiers fall into the river while some boats capsized. Meanwhile, the kosha was picking up speed, and the Mughals understood that the advantage had been lost. However, they wondered why the kosha was speeding towards the Dhaleshwari River when their boats could easily be crushed if the kosha charged at them.

Sona also watched the small fishing boats chase the gigantic kosha from Raj Badi's rooftop. *That's like mice chasing a cat*! she thought with a bemused expression on her face.

Meanwhile, Masum marvelled at Isa's foresight and preparedness. He had seen the morning developments and was astonished by the suddenness of the Mughal onslaught. He had experienced various encounters with the Mughals in the past, both for and against, but he had never witnessed such alacrity and fervour among their soldiers. It was unthinkable that the Mughals would cruise through the night under unknown conditions to surprise the enemy, which meant vanquishing Isa and Masum were the top priority of Shahbaz Khan. He knew lesser mortals would have succumbed at predawn, such was the guile displayed by Shahbaz, but Isa and his lieutenants belonged to a different breed.

Confidence soared in Masum as he saw the kosha speed into the Dhaleshwari, and as he watched the riverbank, he saw Mughal horsemen and artillery position themselves to fire at the ship. But a thousand men were rowing, and the

Mughals had not factored the speed of the kosha. As the Mughals saw the kosha approach, they loaded the cannons, but as the first iron pellet boomed from the shore, the kosha had already left them behind. Canons boomed, but all missed their targets.

Isa smiled at Masum.

"The fun begins now!"

"I can see you are leading them to the Shitalakshya River, wherein you armies will bombard the invaders. But I understand we will meet the confluence soon. Will you stop to draw the enemy towards the Shitalakshya River, or proceed upstream to protect your navy from the Mughal artillery?"

Isa pondered for a minute and replied, "Isn't life about taking risks? We need to draw the adversary into our territory. It is broad daylight now, and we can see the opponent from afar. Thus, we will again anchor where the Shitalakshya meets the Dhaleshwari, and our resistance will originate from there. I have cannons stationed at Khizirpur to decimate the foe!"

As the kosha sped towards Khizirpur, Isa asked Masum, "Masum bhai, can Muslims marry Hindu widows?"

Masum thought for a while and then replied, "Isa, I have not been staying in Bengal for a long time. But in the little time I have been here, I understand that Hindus and Muslims are just like two parallel rivers. Never shall they meet. Further, Hindu widows cremate themselves in their husband's pyre, and I do not know of any living Hindu *bewa*."

"Sona is one."

"Shame on you, Isa mian! How can you even think of marrying Sona? Family honour and prestige are sacrosanct to the Kulin Kayasthas ... and widow remarriage is an anathema to the Hindus. I implore you to forget the idea. You will be twice cursed—one, for asking to marry a widow, and second, for being a Muslim."

"Kedar is my dear friend."

"Kedar may be your friend, but religion and tradition transcend friendship. I have watched the Hindu nobles from close when I was associated with the Bengal Sultanate at Tanda. They would visit the court, pay obeisance to the subahdar, but their womenfolk maintained strict privacy and never appeared in front of the Muslim lords. We understood that in order to maintain communal harmony, we had to keep our distance from upper caste Hindu women. It would be sacrilege if you were caught conversing with one of these Kulin ladies—widow or otherwise. They may not be appearing to wear their religion on their sleeves, but the aristocratic Hindus—behind all their liberalism and openness—are actually deeply rooted to tradition. Have you ever seen any of the womenfolk when you have visited the Sripur Raj Badi? Isa Khan, never make the mistake of approaching Sona to converse with her for it would be considered an insult to her honour!"

Masum paused. He could not help but admire Isa's nonchalance, discussing prospects of marrying a Hindu widow while the Mughals chased them.

As the kosha approached Khizirpur, Isa reflected on Masum's comments, *It would indeed be unwise to approach Chand or Kedar Roy and ask Sona's hand in marriage. I have to think of alternatives, but right now I needed to focus on more important tasks.*

He quickly called out instructions, "*Kaptan*, slow down the kosha! My soldiers need to confront the Mughals. Karimullah, ask the men to disembark and take up position at the *qila*.

It was a two-hour wait as Isa and his troops awaited the enemy under the scorching midday sun, but shortly after noon, they noticed the invader approaching Khizirpur. Shahbaz was slightly dispirited initially, having lost the first-mover advantage, but thought that the swift withdrawal by Isa and his men reflected a nervousness in meeting their army. Shahbaz reasoned that the retreat by the kosha, despite the casualty inflicted on the Mughals, meant that Isa felt their troops lacked the strength of the Mughals and hence were afraid to face them.

Although his cavalry was ineffective in attacking Isa and his men at the confluence of the Padma and Meghna, they would be potent on the narrow Dhaleshwari or the Shitalakshya. Thus, as the fishing boats and the cavalry went in tandem, Shahbaz's hopes soared and he started reflecting on the accolades Abu'l-Fath Jalal-ud-din Muhammad Akbar would bestow on him after he was done with vanquishing upstarts like Isa Khan and Masum Khan Kabuli.

Unfortunately for Shahbaz Khan and the Mughals, they had not undertaken a reconnaissance before following the enemy and were unaware of the fortifications that had been undertaken by Isa in the last few years. As they approached the enemy, confident that their cannons would destroy the kosha and the soldiers on the fishing boats would slaughter the survivors, guns roared from the Khizirpur Fort. Shahbaz was not even aware that Isa possessed cannons, and as the artillery fired and targeted the cavalry and the navy simultaneously, Shahbaz realised he had been worsted in tactical warfare. He understood he had come unprepared and that he had to retreat and undertake another campaign if he wanted to gain favours with Emperor Akbar.

As soldiers fell and the Shitalakshya changed colour into a light hue of red, Shahbaz ordered his soldiers to pull back. Isa ordered the kosha to charge at the enemy. The highly surprised Mughals ran helter-skelter as the kosha charged at their fishing boats.

Sona had been watching the fascinating drama unfold from her terrace with great interest.

Sona pondered, *Why is the kosha chasing the Mughals? How come the tables got reversed*?

Sona had been instructed on warfare strategy by her father from a tender age, and she realised a master strategist was at work here. She rushed down to her father's chamber.

"Baba, please come to the terrace at once. "You must see this! That man who was here earlier is chasing the Mughals!"

She clapped her hands and cackled.

Chand was thrilled.

"That must be Isa Khan. We now have someone who can stand up to the Mughals and defeat them."

He called out for Kedar, "Bhai, come quick, the unimaginable is happening!"

As they waited for Kedar to arrive, Sona stood rooted to the spot. *Isa Khan? Who is he? I absolutely must get a glimpse of this remarkable person. I will go to the ghat at daybreak tomorrow. I am sure I will be able to spot him in his kosha.*

Next day, Sona was up early. She quickly proceeded to the ghat, hid behind a neem tree, and peered at the kosha. There was no sign of any activity on the kosha. *Isa babu, get up. Let me have a good look at you, the vanquisher of the Mughals. I will need to return soon, else someone may spot me here which will not look good!*

As Sona contemplated whether to remain or return, two men grabbed her from behind. She tried to scream, but they stuffed a handkerchief into her mouth, picked her up, blindfolded her, tied her hands and quickly carried her to the riverfront.

Sona wanted to shout out to her father and uncle, but she was choked.

Who will hear me this early in the morning? Who will notice my abduction? I have to save myself!

As wild thoughts raced through Sona's mind, she heard a voice, "All well?"

"*Amigo*, let's go!"

Sona wanted to shout out, "Are you crazy? Do you know who I am? My father and uncle will attack you and torment you till you die!" But her mouth was still stuffed. She could make out that she was put on a boat.

As the boat sailed on the Dhaleshwari, Sona realised people would notice she was missing only during lunchtime. The thought frightened her and she started howling. *I hope I am rescued. These Harmads are savages.*

17

"Sonakando" Fort

As Sona lay petrified in the boat, fearing the worst, someone did spot her.

Isa, despite an evening of celebration, had woken up early. He looked up towards Raj Badi, hoping to catch the sight of the captivating beauty on the terrace. He was disappointed because no one was there. But something else caught his eyes. A couple of fishermen were carrying a white bundle towards a fishing boat. As Isa peered more closely, he saw they were carrying a person.

Could it be Sona? Let me find out!

Isa quickly called out, "Karimullah, quickly get the dinghy ready!" There was no point in chasing with the kosha as the fishing boat could overturn due to the bow waves. Instead, it would be easier to approach the boat on a dinghy. They set sail, with both Isa and Karimullah rowing fiercely.

"Masnad-i-Ala, whom are we chasing?"

Isa shrugged his shoulder.

"I do not know, but I saw a person being abducted from the ghat. From the white cloth the person was wearing, it could be Sona, Chand Roy's daughter!"

Seeing the boat approaching fast, the abductors understood it was only a matter of time before they were confronted. The abductors thought of putting up a resistance; they had been patiently waiting for Sona at the ghat for the last couple of days, ever since they spotted her on the terrace. Such a nubile beauty would fetch them a handsome remuneration in the market. But all hopes of putting up a fight evaporated when they saw Karimullah. They hurriedly took their boat towards the shore, jumped out off the boat, and scuttled into the forest.

The sudden rattle startled Sona. She could make out that the boat had suddenly stopped. *What's happening*?

Suddenly, she felt someone hurriedly untying her hands. As soon as her hands were free, she removed the gag from her mouth and hastily pulled the blindfold from her eyes. She saw herself staring at the grey, penetrating eyes of Isa. Embarassed, she hastily pulled back, hit the edge of the boat and almost tumbled into the river. Only to be saved by Isa's alertness, who moved his arms forward to stop Sona from falling. Sona found herself ensconced in Isa's arms. Her embarrassment knew no bounds.

Isa carefully settled Sona on dry ground.

"My name is Isa Khan and I am a friend of Kedar Roy. I saw you being abducted and I gave a chase to your abductors. Seeing us nearing, they left you and fled."

"Isa babu, I saw you vanquishing the Mughals the other day. We are very proud of you."

Isa smiled.

"Dhanyavad. But we are in a quandary. Since your abductors escaped, there is no way I can prove that you were abducted. If I escort you to Sripur now, people may not believe what transpired because Sanatan babu knows that I am fascinated with you and may spread rumours if he hasn't already. What do we do? And how come, no one in Sripur has noticed your absence!"

Isa is enamoured by me? Am I dreaming? She tried to maintain her composure, and replied, "Oh, since I mostly stay within my room, my absence will not be noticed till lunchtime."

"Masnad-i-Ala, I propose I take Sona didi to Kalaigachha Fort. She can stay there for a few days while we think of a strategy to take her back to Sripur. Meanwhile, you make haste to Sripur to meet Chand Roy and Kedar Roy to appraise them of your recent conquest, and then set sail to Kalaigachha. That way, no one would link you to the abduction of Sona didi."

"Isa babu, I am not sure about this. This will complicate matters for me ..."

"Sona, we need to talk. And we don't have any more time to waste. Let's make haste."

Soon after, Isa set towards Sripur.

Sona woke up at daybreak. She recounted the past twenty-four hours and felt grateful that she was safe. *How is Baba reacting to my absence? What does Isa want to talk to me about?* She had grown up as the apple of her father's eye. Chand had taught her the scriptures and accounting at a young age, much to her mother's consternation.

Deboki used to admonish Chand, "What will you achieve by educating our daughter? No respectable family will want to give their son in marriage with a girl who is more educated than the boy?"

Chand would laugh.

"I am the leading bhuiyan and one of the key leaders of the Kayastha community. Anyone whom Sona marries will be beneath the stature of our family. Sona will be neglected whichever family she marries into, and that will be more to humiliate me. I have decided my son-in-law will be a *ghar jamai*, and I am teaching her administrative affairs so she can ensure her *swami* does not squander our wealth when I am not there!"

True to his words, Chand had married Sona off to the sixteen-year-old son of a local, middle-class, respectable Kayastha family. But at the tender age of nine, Sona was too innocent to understand the duties of a wife. The wedding was an elaborate joyous affair, but on her *phool sojjya* night, when Sona saw her groom Madhav enter her bedroom, she ran off scared to her parents' room.

Deboki had protested, "Sona, go back to your room right now!"

But Chand capitulated, "Sona is too young—give her some days and she will understand."

When his marriage was fixed, Madhav was ridiculed by his friends for being a gold-digger.

"Don't you have any shame? Moving in with your in-laws." They would often mock him.

An unresponsive Sona was the last nail in the coffin. Madhav decided to take a sojourn in the Padma to drive away his blues and seek solace in solitude. Unfortunately, he had the misfortune of being captured, tortured and executed by the Mog marauders who were scouting the neighbourhood to loot the prosperous guests attending the grand wedding.

Next day, as Sona still lay asleep, her parents had been informed that the mutilated body of their son-in-law had been found in a *nouka* adrift near the Sripur Ghat. The only recollection that Sona carried from that eventful morning was of being rudely woken up by a desolate Deboki, her bangles being broken, her sari being torn off and her being dressed in pristine white. She still shuddered on the recollection of their house being surrounded by the villagers, people screaming that she also climb the pyre with her husband, and vaguely remembering how her father argued that the marriage was not consummated. Tears rolled down her eyes as a flood of memories about the traumatising day invaded her mind.

I hope this captivity is a temporary affair.

Yet, as Sona reflected, she realised Isa brought in a different emotion in her. She recollected how she had stepped behind a column to secretly watch him when she saw him glancing at her a few days ago, and how thrilled she was when she saw him driving away the Mughals. She could sense Isa was immensely attracted to her, and last night, she had inserted her fingers in her deep inside while thinking of him, something which was a sacrilege for a widow, and yet was the only physical gratification she could enjoy.

But he is a Muslim. Ma always said that they were the scavengers of the worst kind and not to be trusted.

A popular verse about the pious Vaishnavi Gangaram Moitra came to her mind. He was ostracised by the Hindus because he accepted water from the Muslim maid Bhushona and fed her brother Abdullah rice.

Keno bhai Gangaram, aage kolli heno kaam, keno kheli Bhushonar pani? Ghore dili Abdullah-re bhaat, harite na chhoy paat, tore kishe phire kule aani?

(Hey brother Gangaram, why did you do such a wrong thing as accepting water from a Bhushona? You fed Abdullah rice, the pot must never have touched his plate! How can we accept you back?)

Sona's belly growled.

I am hungry. But eating food prepared, served or even touched by a Muslim could be sacrilege and I could lose my religion.

The room she was staying in was well lit due to the clerestory windows. It was quite a big area, in the shape of a square, and Sona guessed the distance between the walls would be over thirty feet. There was a big chouki in one corner and four low stools placed in the room. A few pillows and linens were kept on the bed, and an earthen pitcher with a tumbler was next to the bed. The wooden door to her room was latched from outside, but there was another opening which led her downstairs to a small cellar which had a water tank and a lavatory.

This must be the residence of Isa.

"I can't even drink water from the pitcher until it is purified by Ganga jal," she cried out in frustration. She shut her eyes, hoping she could catch some sleep to forget her hunger.

Sona must have dozed off for she was woken by a knocking on the door. She sat up and enquired, "Yes, who is it?"

She heard Isa's deep baritone voice.

"It is me, Isa. Can I enter your room?"

Sona quickly got up from the bed, sat down on a stool, adjusted her white sari before giving permission to Isa to enter her room.

Isa had come dressed as a king. His blue turban with an emerald-and sapphire-studded brooch on his forehead caught her attention. His attire, both the top and the churidar, matched the blue colour of his turban, and the thick gold filigree necklace only added splendour to his appearance. He had complemented his appearance with an off-white open-chested sherwani, all of which pronounced elegance.

How could anyone look so handsome! I wish I had been born a Muslim. Matters would not be so complicated then! Sona reflected knitting her eyebrows.

She is so breathtaking beautiful. Isa stood mesmerised.

Isa hesitatingly addressed her, "I hope you are comfortable. You must be hungry. I will fix that immediately. Sona, there's something I need to share with you. Maybe what I am doing is not right. Long back, I had given my soul to someone, but I could never release it from her for she died before we could unite. I see her in you, and I want to live again and want to marry you. I know! I know! My touch is anathema to you. My father was a conservative Hindu and yet he married a Muslim lady because he fell in love with her. I hope you too will fall in love with me."

Isa's heart was wilding throbbing. He felt alive after a very long time.

Sona was stunned into silence.

Isa called out, "Achala, *idhar aao*!"

A young damsel slowly walked into the room. She had a terrified look on her face.

"Achala! Thank god you are here!"

Sona lovingly held Achala's hand. Achala finally smiled.

Ever since Sona became a widow, Chand had employed Achala to look after her. Achala was a couple of years younger to her, and they were soulmates.

She gratefully looked at Isa.

"How did you manage to bring her?"

"I just want you to be comfortable. I thought her presence would give you solace and hence I requested her to come over."

Sona was confused.

"Surely, my father knows by now that you have caught me. He will now invade you to rescue me!"

Isa shook his head.

"No one in your family knows yet."

There was pin-drop silence.

"I know trust is a difficult word, but I hope you will learn to believe me. I am keeping you captive here for exactly seven days; after which I will release you. You will be free to go wherever you want. I have made up my mind to marry you, but you can mull things over. If you reject my proposal,

I'll understand and you'll be set free! I will tell your father that you were captured by the Harmads and that I freed you from their clutches, and we will work out the finer details about this narrative once you have made the decision.

"Meanwhile, Achala will cook your food and fetch your water, and her cousin Durga will run errands for you. I can assure you none of the ingredients will be touched by a Muslim. Also, I will not be locking your doors, and you can bolt them from inside."

"How would you explain my absence for a week?"

"Let me think over this. I am sure I will find a way to create a convincing scenario where your father believes that you were caught by the Harmads and I set you free! Let me take your leave now."

As Isa left the two maidens alone, Sona looked up at Achala and an avalanche of thoughts and questions erupted.

"Now I am held captive by Isa Khan! How are my parents reacting? Baba must be very upset! Will they accept me back? How did Isa manage to reach out to you? Are people insinuating bad things about me? What do I do?"

Unable to find any answers to her questions, Sona started sobbing.

"Didi, did you have any food to eat since you were captured?"

"No, I have not eaten anything since I left home. They offered me food, but I prefer to stay hungry rather than lose my religion!"

"Didi, let me prepare some *ghee-bhaat* for you."

Sona was curious.

"Achala, how do you plan to cook my food where the utensils and water are contaminated by Muslim touch?

Further, I still do not understand how Isa managed to get you here!"

Achala paused before answering, "Didi, when I came up to your room yesterday afternoon and saw you missing, I started wondering where you could be. At that point, I saw my cousin Durga waving at me from the ghat. I quickly went to meet her. She said that you were in danger, and I must quickly come with her. She said that I should carry some ganga jal. On my way here, I heard from Durga that Isa babu had instructed her to fetch me. She also told me that you had been abducted by the Harmads but Isa babu had rescued you. Is that true?"

Hearing this, Sona again started weeping, though Achala failed to understand whether she was crying out of remorse or gratitude.

In haste, Achala blurted, "Do not worry, I know you are hungry and I will prepare food soon. Let me purify all the utensils, while I wait for Durga to bring the rice, ghee and water. You will not be polluted."

For the next seven days, Isa visited Sona at least twice daily, always knocking on her door and asking her permission before entering, and every time he came, Sona burst into tears.

On the seventh day Isa braced himself and asked her, "Your time is up, Sona! What have you decided?"

He did not have much hope. For the past week, whenever Isa visited Sona, she would burst in tears.

What Isa or Achala did not realise was Sona's lament was not for the choice she was going to make. Going back to her father meant she would squander the only glimmer of love and passion she had ever felt, while accepting Isa would compel her to embrace a new religion and forget about her parents and loved ones. Though her father loved her dearly and encouraged her to read and learn, she was sure that if she returned to Sripur, he would banish her to Benares or Haridwar due to the social stigma of being abducted. So, either decision meant she would have to break off ties with her family.

If they accept me back after such an ignominy due to their immense love, they would also welcome me if I were to marry Isa. It makes sense to accept Isa's proposal and start my life anew. I can't live that miserable life any more ... but I don't want to lose out financially.

Finally, Sona let out a loud sigh and burst into tears. The tears were more for her father because she knew he would be devastated either way.

Sona requested Achala to give them some privacy and wait outside.

"Unlike us Hindus where we marry for a lifetime, I understand a Muslim can have four wives and give talaq when he does not fancy a wife any more. Hence, what guarantee do I have that you will not discard me once you have married me?"

Isa was startled by the question. He waited to collect his thoughts and replied, "Yes, it is true that we can have four wives, but our family has retained our Hindu tradition to stay faithful to the one whom we marry. Also, as part of our marriage decree, this fort wherein you were kept captive will henceforth belong to you, as also the land adjacent to this area, including Sonargaon, Narayanganj, Idrakpuri,

Firingibazar, Abdullapur, Mirganj, Serajdikha and Dolaifeni. These are some of the finest areas for producing muslin which means it will be a financial catastrophe for me should I divorce you.

"You are giving all your property to me?"

"No, there is more. Also, these properties still belong to me and will only belong to you when we marry ..."

But then Isa paused.

"You are asking me about your *mahr* ... does that mean you have decided to marry me?"

"Yes, I too want to feel alive again. Moreover, I have now nowhere to go ..."

Isa let out a sigh of relief and grinned widely.

"Seeing you crying all the time, I thought what a grave mistake I had made. In fact, I was planning to name this place Sonakando Fort as an ode to you. You had me fooled."

18

The Nikah

I WONDER HOW A MUSLIM WEDDING *ceremony would be like. Whom do I ask? I don't interact with anyone apart from Achala, Durga and Isa ...*

Sona stood staring out of the window of the Kalaigachha Fort, lost in thought.

Sona had never attended a Muslim wedding. Ever since she became a widow, Sona even stopped attending weddings of her community. It was inauspicious for Hindu widows to attend weddings. Although she was too young when she married to remember her wedding rituals and ceremonies, over the years, Sona had got familiar with various unique Bengali wedding rituals and customs like *aibudo bhaat, gaaye holud, tatta* and *shubho drishti.*

Her impending marriage was causing Sona much anxiety. One day, she asked Achala, "Do you have any idea how Muslim weddings are conducted?"

"Yes, Didi, I saw quite a few of those in our neighbourhood. I have heard that the traditions vary between Ashraf Muslims and Ajlaf Muslims."

"Who are Ashrafs and Ajlafs and how are their wedding traditions different?"

Achala scratched her head.

"Didi, I am not too sure, but I believe Ashrafs are high-caste Muslims. I have never attended any of their weddings, but I have attended the weddings of my Muslim friends who are Ajlafs. Their ceremony is quite similar to ours."

"How did your parents let you attend Muslim weddings? Will you not lose your caste because of such transgressions?"

Achala snickered.

"Does religion feed us? You know, the *gareeb* cannot be bothered by questions of morality and religion. For us, survival is the key, not religion. Anyway, I did not consume any food or drinks at the wedding, so my caste is intact. After all, I work in a Hindu household ..."

She paused and hesitatingly asked, "Didi, if you are thinking of undergoing a Muslim wedding, you will have to convert! Will you change your *naam* in order to marry Isa Khan!"

Sona pondered, *Hmm. Why not? I am marrying a person who is deeply in love with me. I am being given a second chance to start my life afresh. I deserve my share of happiness. And I will claim it!*

"Achala, is Isa an Ashraf or Ajlaf?"

"From what I hear from Durga, Isa's father-in-law is a famous Sufi and a descendant from the highest order of the Mussalman sect. Why don't you just ask him yourself?"

Later in the day when Isa visited Sona to discuss about the witnesses for the wedding, Sona asked, "Do you have some time? I need to discuss something more important."

"My love, I have all the time for you."

Without wasting a breath, Sona drove straight to the point.

"Are you an Ashraf or an Ajlaf? What rituals do we need to perform to solemnise our nikah? I hear they have different wedding rites."

"How do you know about Ashrafs and Ajlafs?"

"I was an upper-caste Hindu, and it is important for me to know whether I am marrying into an upper-caste or lower-caste Muslim family."

"My pitaji was an orthodox Hindu, probably enjoying a much higher social standing vis-à-vis your family. Yet, he converted to Islam to marry his lady love. I am an Ajlaf because he was a convert. But I am the ruler of Sonargaon and you will be the rani. So, it is not for you to wonder how society will treat you, but rather for you to think how you want to treat your subjects! As for what rituals will be followed, I am at a loss here for I was married when I was young and do not have any recollections, and I have never actually participated in a traditional wedding since."

Sona smiled.

"That makes two of us. I do not want to make any faux pas on the wedding day because rituals matter and need to be carried out correctly."

Isa reflected on Sona's request and commented, "My wife Fatima is currently staying at the Goaldi Mosque. Why don't you visit her and ask her?"

Sona was aghast.

"Your first wife is alive? I thought she had died, for did you not tell me that in your culture too, husbands stay faithful to their wives? Now, you tell me that you have another *biwi*, and you have the insolence to ask me to go and visit her! Do you understand how humiliating it is for both of us?"

"We are cousins actually, and she is more a friend than a wife. We have not slept together for a long time. Fatima will appreciate that you have approached her and will accept you willingly. After all, you should understand that she comes from a culture which believes that a *mard* can have four wives. In fact, she will be grateful if you reach out to her because it means you are respecting her as the elder wife!"

She glared at Isa and hissed, "I am no Fatima bibi, I am the daughter of a Kulin Kayastha, an educated Kshatriya! Personal honour is most important to me, and hell has no fury as a Kshatriya woman disgraced! Isa mian, you have been warned. Never think of marrying another woman!"

He grinned and added, "When I have found my *sona* bibi, why should I look elsewhere? However, if I ever take another wife, she will serve you and be your *dashi*."

Sona was not amused.

"I already have two servants and if I need more, I will hire them!"

Isa tried to hold her hand, but Sona brushed it off.

She composed herself and said, "From the tradition from where I come, marriage is between two families, and it is a life-term commitment to be carried on for seven lifetimes. But whatever I have understood about Islamic marriage, it is a contract and can be nulled and made void any time by the husband by repeating talaq thrice. Do you not feel it is demeaning to a woman to annul a marriage like that? You will either belong to me or to no one else!"

Isa was puzzled.

"Are you sure Hindu men can have only one wife? I have seen so many instances were Brahmin men have dozens of wives, each in a different village?"

Sona bit her tongue, *He is right*. "I do not want to get into a debate with you. You have been warned! I now look forward to meeting Fatima didi."

True to her words, Sona went to meet Fatima who embraced her and said, "Ever since my mian returned from Turan, I always heard him recounting Pari's name whenever we made love. It disgusted me, but today I can see why he was so madly in love with her. He tells me, you are a splitting image of Pari. Anyone would fall in love with such a beautiful maiden like you."

Sona smiled.

"Didi, you are too kind to me. Thank you for the compliments. I have so many questions to ask you. Do I need to wear a burqa like you?"

Fatima instantly took off her niqab. Sona was staring into the face of an elderly woman, someone who reminded her of her mother, and understood why Isa felt the need for romance.

"This is a niqab, not a burqa. As to whether to wear it or not, it is your personal decision. My father says wearing a niqab is not obligatory."

She touched Fatima's feet. "Didi, I am young and unaccustomed to your culture. Please tell me about your wedding rituals. I don't want to take a misstep and invite misfortune into my life again. I am taking a big step and there's no turning back. I need to get everything right."

Fatima smiled and nodded.

"I understand. The Ajlafs, have continued with a few Hindu traditions like gaaye holud, tatta, bou bhaat. The one tradition that is different from a Hindu wedding ceremony is the *rusmat*, which is similar to your shubho drishti, but here the *dulhan* and the *dulha* look at each other through a mirror and describe to the guests what they are seeing!"

Sona smiled.

"That sounds like a lot of fun!"

"Not necessarily. When I married my cousin and was told to describe what I saw in the mirror, I innocently said, '*Ibn al khaal*' and the guests all started laughing."

Sona gave her a blank stare.

"Why?"

"It is the Persian equivalent of maternal cousin."

Sona giggled.

"You called your husband *mastuto bhai* on your wedding day!"

"Sona, what rituals you follow is not important. But what is important is to respect the traditions and culture of the place where you will rule. I have been in Sonargaon for a long time now, and I have learnt a lot about this place from *Abbujan*. I would like to educate you about Sonargaon so that you are a worthy *malkah* here!"

Over the next few days, Fatima escorted Sona through the villages of Aminpur, Pannam, Goaldi and Moghrapara, recounted the illustrious history of the ancient city of Sonargaon, and how it developed as a religious town where pirs and fakirs congregated.

One day they visited the Panch Pir dargah, "Most importantly, Sonargaon is the town of the five pirs! They have long died, but their memories are kept alive by Muslims and Hindus, especially the sailors who come to pay their respects at this tomb." Sona noticed a piece of iron, resembling a human head and five fingers resembling the five pirs, mounted on the graves.

Fatima also escorted Sona to the nameless grave at Moghrapara which had a thick coating of lime.

"Everyone comes here to identify the thief whenever a theft is committed. You need to place your hand on the tomb and swear your innocence, and if you are lying, your hand gets stuck tightly to the lime."

"Didi, whatever you have been showing me is associated with the pirs. Sonargaon is such an old inhabitation, surely, there must be Hindu and Buddhist relics too!"

"The new makes way for the old. Only one ancient Hindu relic exists, the Jhikoti. I am not aware of its history, though the Hindus meet there for prayers often."

As Sona spent the next few days exploring Sonargaon, she stopped feeling less anxious about the new people and the place. Before the day of the wedding, Fatima advised Sona, "Sonargaon is famous for its muslin, and people visit here to buy this exquisite cloth which is so smooth that it can pass through a ring. I have even heard that merchants place this fabric in hollow bamboos and carry them to Khurasan, Persia, Turkey and Europe. I implore you to wear a *mulmul* sari as a token of appreciation to the skilled artisans who reside in your kingdom."

On the wedding day, Sona wore a pristine white muslin dress for her nikah, was rechristened as Niyamat Jaan by the qazi and enthusiastically said, "*Mujhe qubool hai*" to solemnise her marriage to Isa Khan.

At the rusmat ceremony, when the guests enquired what the two had seen in the mirror, Isa said, "A fairy!"

"*Chor*—someone who has stolen my heart!"

Thus, as fun and gaiety filled the room and celebrations erupted in Sonargaon, news reached Chand Roy that his beloved Sona was now married to a Muslim. Chand immediately summoned Kedar and said, "How did this happen? How could they meet? Was Sona forced into this marriage? This is a slap to our community. Kedar, do not spare Isa, he needs to die!"

Meanwhile, Sona was most perturbed about the phool sojjya, having recollections from her early childhood of being pushed into a flower-laden room and running off from there, which led to disastrous consequences. When the couple was alone in their room, Isa looked into Sona's eyes and gently said, "You are Niyamat Jaan to the world, for others you are Sona, but for me, you are Sona Bibi. My golden wife. Would you conquer all obstacles along with me?"

"Jaan, from this day, I am your heart and pulse. Nothing can separate us!"

As she said those words, Sona found Isa trying to kiss her. She had never been kissed, but she felt good because it felt exquisite. As she reached out to embrace Isa, she could feel his stiffness. Sona felt embarrassed and shy.

Isa's beard and moustache was tickling her, and she started giggling.

Isa was puzzled. "Why are you giggling?"

"You are tickling me!"

"I will tickle you more."

Isa climbed on Sona and started tickling her, and Sona also started tickling him, and as they started jostling, Isa entered her.

She moaned.

"Isa, what are you doing?"

Isa licked her lower lips, pressed her breasts and said, "What I have been wanting to do for a long time."

"I want more ...!"

As they reached the climax, both hoped tomorrow would never come.

19

The Test

"Saheb, wake up! Wake up Sona didi!"

Isa woke with a start.

"What happened, Achala?"

"Saheb, Karimullah wants to urgently discuss something with you!"

Isa quickly planted a kiss on Sona's forehead and dashed out.

As Sona lay in her bed soaking in the morning sunlight, she smiled to herself. She felt lucky and blessed to have married Isa. As a widow, she had been wearing plain white cotton sarees, maintaining short hair, applying no make-up on her face, and eating a strict vegetarian affair where even garlic and onion were taboo. Not just that, she could not consume many vegetables or masoor dal as these were considered to increase one's sexual desires which a widow could ill afford.

She pondered, *How things have changed now. I can not only wear colourful silk or muslin sarees, but also salwar-kurtas and gowns. Though wearing sarees at home makes it so much easier to make love ...*

She blushed thinking about last night. Isa poured cold fermented date juice on her breasts. As it trickled down her midriff, down to her navel and further below, Sona shivered. Isa licked her clean, which again made Sona long for more, though now her breasts ached and her insides felt sore. As Isa entered her again, they locked their lips, gulped down the juice, hugged each other tightly and crashed intoxicated.

Sona had now started taking good care of herself too. She no longer went for an early morning dip, though she believed she could still chant the one hundred and eight names of Ganga if she wanted to. Instead, Isa's begum would have Achala give her a relaxing body massage and apply coconut oil on her hair following which Sona would take a luxurious bath in rose water daily.

Today, she knew that Isa would not return before lunch, so Sona called out, "Achala, quickly heat the water. I want to wash my hair with *reetha*."

As Achala was scrubbing Sona's neck with *multani mitti*, she remarked, "Didi, you are becoming more beautiful by the day. You were always fair, but now you are milk-white. You also have put on weight in all the right places and your breasts are fuller! Marriage does this!"

Sona feigned sleep, pretending she had not heard Achala.

Sona could see that she was undergoing a physical transformation. *But is it due to the intense passionate lovemaking I am enjoying each night?* she contemplated. *Maybe Achala is right.* She smiled to herself as she thought about Isa's passionate lovemaking almost every night, as if there was no tomorrow, and it was only when both were exhausted that they would finally try to drift off to sleep. But her chain of thoughts was broken as she realised Achala was staring at her.

"Why are you looking at me like that?"

"Didi, you never reacted to what I said!"

"Sorry, your *maalish* was so relaxing that I must have dozed off. What did you say?"

Achala repeated what she had said earlier, and grinned.

"Have I put on weight? Do I look really *mota* now?"

Sona was worried.

"Isa mian comes in so late, and then he is so tired, that he immediately goes off to sleep. So, it is not what you think. I do not think shaadi is the reason behind my putting on weight. It must be the change in diet.

"Ma always used to say '*Hindu jokhon musalman hoy, gorur jom hoy* (When a Hindu converts to Islam, he becomes a cow's devil)!' But only when you taste beef do you realise how succulent and tasty it is, especially when it is mixed with ginger, garlic, onion and black pepper, slow-cooked overnight over the fire. I have heard eating beef makes you bigger and stronger. Also, I partake of meals as often as I wish. But it is good that you have noticed it, for now onwards, I will restrict my food intake."

Sona asked Achala to wait, saying she would return after a quick bath, so that Achala could apply kajal on her eyes, tie false hair and make her hair into a bun.

The talk on food had made Achala curious, so when Sona returned and she started inserting pins in her hair, she asked Sona, "Didi, I hear the Harmads are trying to introduce several new vegetables here. Have you tried any of those?"

Sona remembered the time when the Portuguese generals of Isa's army had visited them and brought a few exotic vegetables with them.

"I remember the firangis once brought a purplish vegetable which they called *vilayeti begun*. We roasted it, rubbed mustard oil and salt and and it tasted really nice.

Then there was this white-coloured oval vegetable, something similar to our *gathi kochu,* which they called batata. It was boiled and served, along with salt and this chopped green-colour vegetable resembling a tiny shrivelled banana, and my mouth was literally on fire. It was so tasty. I wanted to have more, and these firangis advised me to drown the pungency with wine, so I was quite drunk by the time the meal was over. I do not remember much of that evening, but I hope I did not embarrass Isa mian."

She paused and added, "Achala, I am happy about the choices I made otherwise I would have simply survived on ghee-bhaat for the rest of my life."

Achala smiled.

"Didi, I can see that this life is suiting you. Your beauty has blossomed, your skin glows, and every passing day I can feel you are more relaxed!"

However, even as Achala spoke these words, Sona knew that she might be happy, but she was worried. She was troubled primarily because Isa was perturbed. Quite often, late in the night, when both she and Isa were deeply asleep, the frequent calls of the bugle would wake them up and Isa would hurriedly dress and scamper to see the source of the disruptions. While Isa never mentioned the reason behind these distractions, Sona gathered from Achala that Kedar Roy was the reason behind these disturbances.

Isa's forts across Sonargaon and Narayanganj were heavily protected, and Kedar knew that it would be difficult to attack them in broad daylight, so he usually attacked these at night to catch Isa's men unawares. She sighed as she pondered, *We need to either attack Sripur or leave Sonargaon.*

Yet, when Sona discussed this with Isa, he replied, "Your father and uncle helped me to consolidate my position in Bhati, and look how I repaid their trust by marrying you. They have a reason to attack me, but I cannot launch an attack on Sripur because that would antagonise the other bhuiyans. If I do not attack and simply defend myself, all the zamindars will realise that while I have erred in falling in love with you, I am repentant but not vindictive and can be trusted for the unification of Bengal.

"Also, the question of abandoning Sonargaon does not arise as it is one of the most prosperous regions. Places like Sonargaon, Sripur and Chandradwip are easy to defend and difficult to attack. Just as it would be foolhardy for me to attack Sripur as I would be caught in the line of their cannons, so it would be unwise of your uncle to attack me if his position was revealed. The bugle sounds are more to warn him and his men that their movements have been spotted, and we just let loose a few arrows so that they retreat."

"If the bugle sounds are false alarms, why do you have to leave whenever they play?"

Isa smiled.

"It is always better to be safe than sorry!"

Sona was also bothered for one more reason. It was now almost a few weeks since she had missed her period. She thought worriedly, *These are trying times, I hope I have not conceived. Maybe my weight gain, weariness and irritability are because of that.*

Sona decided to visit the hakim. As Sona changed into a salwar-kurta and clipped a veil on her forehead, Achala asked, "Didi, where are you going?"

"You ask too many questions. Please change and come with me."

As she waited for Achala to get ready, Sona felt uneasy, ran to the bathroom and threw up the puffed rice she had eaten in the morning.

Finally, Sona stepped out with Achala from their red double-storey mansion which stood adjacent to a large lake.

"Ah! What a pleasant summer morning, Achala!"

"Yes, Didi, but why are the streets empty?

Sona was intrigued for Sonargaon was always bustling with activity during daytime, especially before noon, so that people could retreat indoors to escape from the scorching afternoon sun. She found a few people surreptitiously running with their belongings as if to escape the place.

"What's going on? Why is there so much of commotion, Achala?

Achala wore a confused expression on her face.

Sona could sense trouble was brewing. *I wish Fatima didi was here and not in Sarail. She always had the pulse of the community*. Wondering what was happening, Sona trudged to the hakim's place.

The hakim rushed out on seeing her. "Niyamat bibi, I hope everything is well. The morning has been very hectic, with people rushing here to pick up medicines before leaving town."

"What is happening, Hakim mian?"

The hakim, an elderly, bearded man with a shrivelled face, was unsure.

"I heard that the fort of Khizirpur has been attacked, that women are being raped, and men and children are being slaughtered ..."

"My uncle could never do that! His enmity is with my husband, not the villagers!"

The hakim smiled.

"Niyamat bibi, I never once suggested that your *chacha* is behind all this. Maybe it is the Mogs or the Mughals! You should know better as I hear Isa mian has ordered the town to be evacuated. But hurry, tell me, what bothers you?"

Sona did not know how to broach the subject with the hakim, so hesitatingly said, "I have been feeling lethargic lately and even vomited today!"

"When did you last have your period?"

"Maybe around eight or nine weeks back."

The hakim said, "Hmm. We will shortly find out what's troubling you."

He called out to his wife.

The hakim's wife, a pleasant-looking middle-aged woman with warm, green eyes and a lantern jaw, stepped out, listened to her husband and then escorted Sona inside the house.

She handed a glass bottle to Sona and said, "Please urinate inside it."

Once Sona had emptied herself, the hakim's wife studied the colour and the characteristics of the urine and poured some wine into the bottle.

"Please lie down, Niyamat bibi."

Sona did as asked and the elderly woman examined her vagina.

"Come, let's step outside. I need to show the urine to my husband."

The hakim observed the bottle, picked some peas, planted them in the soil and poured the contents of the bottle on the soil around the peas.

"What is your diagnosis, Bibi?"

"Niyamat bibi, congratulations! You are going to become a mother soon. Your insides have a purple-red hue, which along with the texture of your urine, confirms that you are pregnant."

The hakim nodded in concurrence.

"How confident are you that I am pregnant?"

"I am reasonably confident, but we can confirm in four-five days, after studying the growth of the peas. But if you want to know quicker, you can insert an onion in your vagina tonight and check if your mouth smells of onion in the morning. Should you get no smell in your mouth, it means you are pregnant."

What if the onion slips inside my body? Sona shuddered at the thought.

"Hakim mian, I shall visit you after another five days. *Khuda hafiz.*"

As the women walked back home, a cannon boomed. Sona looked out towards the source of the sound and spotted fire balls at a distance. *Has the Khizirpur Fort fallen?* As the maddening thought crossed Sona's mind, she almost sprinted home.

"Didi, don't run!"

As they crossed the Goaldi Mosque, Sona encountered Isa with a retinue of his soldiers. "Where have you been? We were desperately searching for you. We need to vacate Sonargaon immediately and flee on our kosha."

Before Sona could respond, Isa hurried towards the port, almost dragging Sona with him.

"Isa, what is happening?"

"The Mughals have attacked. Shahbaz Khan is on us!"

20

The Messenger

AS THE KOSHA SAILED UPSTREAM along the Meghna towards Sarail, Sona felt famished. Before visiting the hakim, she had left instructions to the cook that rice, *egg bhujia,* minced beef curry, fried *parwal,* dal and *payesh* be prepared for lunch. She had been looking forward to her lunch with Isa and planning to break the good news. *Uff, all plans have gone for a toss! I am sure the servants are probably having a feast now.* As she thought about the delicacies she could have enjoyed, Sona became irritable.

"Till the other day, you were raving about the fortified defences of Sonargaon, how the rivers and the forts protected the town, and today, at the sight of the Mughal army, you scooted the place! If Sonargaon is so well protected, I do not understand why we had to leave it!"

Isa could see Sona was upset. Most people would be fretful when fleeing a battlefield and would have been irritated by the question, but Isa was made of sterner stuff. He reflected on Sona's query and replied, "It is true that Sonargaon is strategically located. But my men were busy keeping a watch on Kedar Roy and his men and we failed to anticipate Shahbaz's movements. It was a covert operation carefully planned.

"My informants appraised me three days back that the Mughals were heading towards Pabna to attack Masum Khan, but last evening, they changed their course and in the middle of the night, a part of the army covered one fifty kosh and surrounded Khizirpur Fort before dawn. Our men were busy keeping a watch on the southern side towards Sripur, while our enemy moved swiftly from the west. I must admire Shahbaz's planning as yesterday was *amavasya* and it would have been difficult to detect their movements even if we had been vigilant.

"Surely, the swift movement of the horses would have been heard by the villagers in Makoan and Mirkadim and they would have alerted our army!"

Isa grimaced.

"From what I hear, families have been massacred in these villages so that they could not forewarn us. Shahbaz's tactics remind me of Genghis Khan. I gather Shahbaz travelled from the Padma bank near Pabna with five hundred of his swiftest horsemen so that he could arrive before dawn, and as the sun emerged, our troops realised that the Khizirpur Fort was surrounded.

"We could not fire at the enemy from Kalaigachha as the Khizirpur Fort stood in the line of fire, while cannons could not be fired from Khizirpur as the enemy was below the fort. We hoped our archers could inflict casualties on the Mughals, but a hundred archers are ineffective against soldiers wearing chain mail and plate armour. I watched elephants prise open the entrance doors of the Khizirpur Fort. I was baffled as to how the elephants came so quickly from Pabna, but my spies have now informed me that they were supplied by Chand Ghazi of Chandpratap!

"Thankfully, most of my men could escape from the fort as we provided cover to them by firing guns at the enemy—a few were killed—but the Mughals quickly took possession of Khizirpur and pointed the cannons at our direction. I thought this would become a battle of attrition between the two forts, till one was demolished, but since the mortar shelling would lead to significant casualties of ordinary citizens, I ordered the town to be evacuated. I had hoped to attack Khizirpur Fort tonight through the secret tunnel on its northern side, though I was worried that we would be caught on two flanks if Kedar Roy decided to attack us at Sonargaon tonight.

"Then I noticed the dust at the horizon and realised Shahbaz's main army was now joining the attack. I believe his army has over ten thousand soldiers. Their cannons are also modern and more powerful. With Khizirpur Fort captured, the Mughals can now fire at us from across the Shitalakshya River and inflict significant damage on us. I therefore decided to retreat and preserve my strengths and ambush Shahbaz later when he is unprepared. Though some of my men continue to be stationed at the forts of Katrabo and Idrakpuri from where they will defend their positions. But let us not waste time talking; lunch must have been served and let us enjoy it!"

Meals in the army usually meant either khichri or biriyani. The cook had hastily cooked mutton biriyani because it was a dish consumed by both Hindus and Muslims. Beef was untouchable by the Hindus, pork by Muslims, whereas chicken was supposed to cause leprosy.

As they sat down for lunch, Karimullah rushed in with a few green chillies.

"Begum, here have these. I know how much you enjoy them!"

Sona smiled, picked up one, bit the chilly and dug into her food.

"The biryani tastes divine with these chillies!"

She was thankful for having missed her lunch. Karimullah asked, "Masnad-i-Ala, what is our plan?"

Isa thought for a while and then answered, "I do not think we have the wherewithal to oppose Shahbaz now. We need to hold on for another few weeks, by which time the monsoon will descend, and then we will confront our enemy. In the meantime, we need to give a suitable response to Chand Ghazi of Gazipur. The troops, including me, will disembark shortly at Karimpur Ghat and make our way to Bhawal. I need to know where Fazl Ghazi's loyalties lie before heading for Chandpratap.

"In the meantime, please stay back with five hundred soldiers on the kosha and escort the women and children to Sarail. Thereafter return to Sonargaon quickly, but in stealth. I expect Shahbaz to depart for Chandpratap when he hears that I have attacked Fazl Ghazi, and we should recapture Sonargaon as soon as he leaves. After annexing Sonargaon, repair the damaged forts and wait for my further instructions. Remember, we may have retreated but a battle is never won until the last man has fallen!"

As the kosha slowed down, Sona realised that they must have neared Karimpur. She was in two minds, whether to let Isa know about her condition. *I don't want him to worry too much. But he needs to know! And now is the time!* As Isa was about to disembark, he realised Sona was not around.

"Achala, where is bibi?"

"Didi just went indoors!"

Isa went inside to bid goodbye to his begum. He said, "I know you must be feeling miserable as this is the first time you are staying away from me. But sometimes we need to go to wars and as my consort, it is your duty to come and stand behind all the soldiers and give them moral support. You should not allow your tensions and worries to affect our troops. Do not worry, you will feel at home in Sarail with Musa and Fatima."

"I am not feeling sad because you are going to battle. I am feeling sad since I have not shared an important news with you."

Isa was confused.

"Pray, what may that be?"

"You are going to become a father soon. But we can celebrate when you return victorious from the *jung*. Now, let us go and let me bid farewell to my brave men!"

Isa was stunned. *Is Sona joking? How could she keep away such a joyous news from me? I wish we had some time to spend together.* As the thoughts buzzed in his mind, he turned ecstatic. He enthusiastically hugged Sona and said, "This is the most wonderful news you could have shared with me. I wish we could celebrate now! When did you find out? From when have you been missing your period? Is it confirmed? Is your health fine? You now need to take more care of yourself!"

Sona winked.

"I came to know today morning but now who is forgetting his soldiers?"

Isa was at a loss of words for once. He composed himself.

"This is such a good news that I now want to spend all my time next to your side till our child is born. Alas, duty beckons. Let me enjoy your company for a few more minutes. My soldiers will not begrudge me that!"

Meanwhile, Shahbaz Khan was surprised to see Isa's sudden retreat. He had not expected the courageous Isa to abandon Sonargaon so easily. As he recollected his past encounter with Isa, he wondered whether the master strategist was up to something. He contemplated whether to cross the Shitalakshya River with his entire army and then await Isa's counterattack or undertake a recce first in Sonargaon with a smaller army. After much deliberation, he decided to move his entire troop to Sonargaon but in batches.

The distance between Kalaigachha Fort and Sonargaon was hardly twenty-four kilometres, and it was late in the afternoon when he approached Isa's mansion. Shahbaz Khan had heard that Sonargaon was the second capital of Bengal after Gaur, but it was nowhere as splendid as the erstwhile capital. He was surprised to see no townsfolk around and pondered how the town could have been emptied out so quickly unless the leader enjoyed the trust and the confidence of his people so as to follow his evacuation order blindly. Once bitten, twice shy! Shahbaz halted to have a good view of his surroundings. His eyes glanced towards the Katrabo Fort, and he had the feeling that people were watching him from the citadel. He decided to withdraw for the night and start afresh tomorrow.

Meanwhile, Kedar Roy heard about the skirmishes at Kalaigachha and felt it was an opportune moment to make another attempt at Sonargaon. He decided to attack through the Shitalakshya River as the Mughals and Isa Khan's army would be busy maintaining vigil on each other, but he was unaware that the Kalaigachha Fort had been abandoned by Isa Khan. As they disembarked on the banks of the Shitalakshya River and Kedar stepped out of the goyna, a cannon roared, and the projectile landed on the boat. Kedar turned back and looked in aghast as the severed bodies of four of his companions floated on the river. Kedar and his men turned back, running for shelter, as more guns roared in the horizon. Kedar realised retreat was better and he and his army scampered back to Sripur.

It was early morning when Kedar and his men reached Sripur. Chand Roy had just finished his morning prayer at the Tara temple, and seeing a bloodstained Kedar alighting from the boat, rushed to the riverfront. "I hope you are fine, Kedar. Did you manage to avenge the loss of our pride?"

"I am fine, Dada, but I have lost some of my men. All these days we have been proceeding towards Sonargaon, not a single shot was fired at us but today, cannons were fired at us from the Kalaigachha Fort. I hear that the Mughals have occupied it, and they are firing indiscriminately. They must be desperate!

"Dada, I have no love lost for Isa for marrying Sona. It is a slap on the face of the Kulin Kayasthas of Bikrampur—the Guhas, Ghoshes and Basus, but I must appreciate his stance of not attacking us when we tried to raid Sonargaon. We need to put aside our differences, as the Mughals are our greater enemies. If Isa succumbs, Shahbaz Khan may then train his eyes on Sripur. I have also heard how Shahbaz has annihilated villages on his march towards Sonargaon. The rural folk are complaining, saying that we are a mere spectator while Shahbaz plunders Bhati."

"How can you forgive Isa for what he did to us? I cannot live if we are unable to take revenge on Isa Khan!"

Kedar contemplated for a while before answering.

"Dada, we will confront Isa at a later date. We need to now consolidate our resistance and support him. Let me reassure you that ours will be a strategic alliance though I will not forgive or forget the embarrassment they have caused, and we will extract our revenge later."

"Kedar, I hear Isa has fled Sonargaon. I think the Mughals will now chase him. Let us see how he fares against the Mughals this time. If he resists the Mughals successfully, we can then think of supporting him. For the time being, let us wait and watch. As it is, we can defend Sripur well, but attack is not our forte!"

Kedar nodded.

"What you say makes sense."

As the brothers proceeded towards Raj Badi, the guns boomed in the distant horizon.

Shahbaz had sent a team out for inspection in the night, who had confirmed that soldiers were present in the forts of Katrabo and Idrakpuri. The fort of Katrabo was in the vicinity of Sonargaon and it had to be captured if the Mughals were to roam freely in the town. So, at night-time, the cannons were moved and positioned near the fort, and at daybreak, the projectiles were targeted at the fort gate.

The sentries at the fort had noticed the enemy at dawn, and rushed to inform Rakhal, who was now commanding the fort. Rakhal ran upstairs, urging his men to set up the cannons, but even as he shouted, the first cannonball hit the wall and the entire fort vibrated. The reverberations sent a chill down his spine. Shots were fired in unison and Rakhal realised they could not hold on to the fort. He ordered, "Let the sentries stay with me and we will fire a few shots at the Mughals to distract them, while the rest of you escape through the tunnel and flee."

But as Rakhal and his three sentries mounted the cannons, the Mughals directed their cannons towards them. Rakhal noticed the fireballs approaching him. One of the shots landed on the cannon and a deafening explosion roared through Sonargaon, stifling the agonised cries of Rakhal. Thus, when Shahbaz triumphantly entered the citadel, he was puzzled to see no one inside the fort, except for four disfigured, charred bodies on the tower keep. As he wondered where the soldiers could have escaped, he was informed that an envoy had come from Gazipur to meet him.

"Subahdar, I am coming from Chandpratap. Chand Ghazi is no more. Isa Khan attacked us in the night and ransacked our province, openly declaring that this was a warning to anyone who sided with the *shatru* and betrayed the Bengalis."

Shahbaz thundered, "Gazipur is only forty-five kilometres from here. If we make haste, we can reach there in two hours. Isa and his men should be resting after the night-long siege, and we can catch them unawares. Three thousand of my horsemen will come with me, while the rest of my army can follow at their pace, though five hundred soldiers will stay back in Sonargaon and ensure that Isa does not sneak back here while I am attacking him in Gazipur."

Then, to reassure himself and his men, he roared, "Isa, you cursed child of a mangled dog, your end is near!"

21

The Seige of Jongol Badi

As the sun rose in the morning, Isa thought about the carnage in Chandpratap. He, along with his army was approaching Karimpur Ghat, and he now needed to decide his next course of action. Isa abhorred violence and bloodshed always reminded him of the slaughter of his father and brother. *Yet, war was a necessary evil and conspirators had to be punished.* Thus, when he had visited Fazl Ghazi of Bhawal yesterday afternoon, Isa directly asked, "Fazl mian, Allah says that in Islam, every life is important. Yet I desire to take the lives of certain people. I wanted your opinion on the same."

Fazl became alarmed.

"Oh no, Isa mian, what have I done?"

Isa laughed.

"No, I was not talking about you but about your *padosi*, Chand Ghazi!"

Fazl relaxed.

"Chand is a distant cousin and we all hail descendancy from Pahlwan Shah who came to this region almost two hundred and fifty years ago for preaching Islam. I do not want to speak bad about Chand, but I believe he is hobnobbing with the Mughal subahdar and reporting our activities back to the emperor. He frequently visits Tanda, and I suspect he provides feedback on the crop output in our region, for how else does the subahdar know the amount of khazna we need to pay."

Isa reflected.

"What you say makes sense. I hear lots of innocent villagers were slaughtered when Shahbaz raided Sonargaon. I was wondering why he went on a rampage, but now I believe Shahbaz must have known that the villagers would beat the drums and I would be forewarned, and hence they were exterminated. But why do you continue to pay taxes to the Mughals?"

Fazl sheepishly grinned.

"Isa mian, I do not have a big army or the natural advantages to defend Bhawal. Therefore, I pay a decorum of taxes to ensure I am not attacked. But Inshallah, you defeat the Mughals, and I will stop paying taxes, revolt against them and instead pay you taxes!"

Isa smiled.

"So you also endorse attacking Chand Ghazi."

Fazl Ghazi nodded in acquiescence. Isa did not want to lose any more time, so he ordered his army to camp but gathered a few of his trusted lieutenants and informed them, "Betrayal begets blood! We shall attack the Chandpratap palace tonight. Remember, our enmity is with Chand Ghazi and not the villagers, so we will not harm them. But we need to be careful so that the villagers do not raise any alarm."

Isa and his men waited for night to descend on the tranquil province of Gazipur. It was summer, when village folks prefer to sleep outside on their charpoy under the cool evening air, and thus they could not carry lighted torches with them. Isa advised his men to carry smouldering embers in earthen pots, and under the dark summer night, they quietly proceeded to Chand Ghazi's mansion. They tied their horses behind the trees when they were in the vicinity of the mansion and hid in the flower bushes. Chand's residence was dark, though the lights were on in a couple of bedchambers.

Isa thought *Chand must be in one of those rooms, enjoying the night with his favourite begum or londi.*

There were two sentries in the front portico, but both fell in unison as a sheaf of arrows descended on them. Isa looked around, but there seemed to be no one around. The absence of an army surprised Isa, and then he reflected *Chand must have sent his army with the elephants to Sonargaon.* Isa and his men surreptitiously surrounded the building, poured oil all along the perimeter, locked the exit doors and set fire to Chand Ghazi's mansion. Then they retreated behind the trees, mounted their horses and waited.

It was the peak of the dry, scorched summer and the fire caught on rapidly. The building was soon engulfed in fire, which alerted one of the soldiers in the barracks. Soon, a troop came running, but they were confused and did not know what steps to take. Someone shouted, "Throw buckets of water!" Everyone ran to their barracks to pick up buckets and fill them with water, but to no avail.

Chand Ghazi was in bed with his favourite courtesan Meena Bai, thinking about the largesse Shahbaz Khan would shower on him for his successful campaign against Isa Khan, when he realised something was not right. There was a strong smell of camphor, and then he realised the building was on fire. He shouted, "*Aag*! *Aag*! *Bachao*!" But he could not decide which direction to take as the fire was all around. The gut-wrenching shrieks of Chand and his dear ones filled the night air as the blaze engulfed the residents. Isa came out from behind the trees, and bellowed, "Let this be a warning to anyone who betrays Bhati!"

After obliterating Chand, Isa contemplated, *Should I camp in Gazipur? But I am sure Shahbaz would raid it at the earliest. It would be imprudent to lock horns with Shahbaz in an open area as there would be unnecessary spillage of blood.*

He finally decided to camp with his army at Karimpur Ghat. Isa sent an emissary to Chatmohar in Pabna, requesting Masum Khan Lohani for reinforcements. He was excited ever since Sona mentioned yesterday that she was pregnant. *Do I visit Sarail, retreat and recapture Sonargaon, or travel upwards across the Meghna?*

Visiting Sarail was risky because if Shahbaz attacked it, Musa, Fatima, Sona and their unborn child would be exposed to danger. Karimullah was already on his way back to regain Sonargaon, but its forts needed to be repaired, and if Isa returned there and there was a Mughal onslaught, it would be difficult to defend the region. Isa finally decided that it would be best to move upwards into the Bhati region, away from Sarail, so that he could entice Shahbaz to follow him, and wait for reinforcements from Masum Khan before confronting him. Isa pondered, *Shahbaz would pursue me with his cavalry, while his artillery would follow later, and thus, it would be judicious to meet the Mughals when Masum's men joined me with their muskets.*

Shortly after noon, one of Isa's spies came and informed him, "Saheb, Shahbaz with over three thousand of his men is moving at lightning speed towards Gazipur."

Isa immediately accumulated his men.

"I do not want to confront the Mughals, for surely after they see the mayhem at Chandpratap, they will ride out here. We need to exit fast from this place, for if we face them now, probably we will win, but there will be bloodshed. I do not want to lose my people. Hence, I want the Mughals to follow us, and we will meet them when the muskets arrive from Pabna. We will proceed towards Kishoreganj, wait for the Mughals to attack and then take stock of the situation. We leave now and travel tonight, so that we can be at Kishoreganj by daybreak."

As morning approached, it appeared to Isa that they had left the plains of Bengal and her paddy fields and were entering an impenetrable jungle. It reminded him of Sarail when he had first arrived. There were few peasants visible, and Isa asked, "What is this land called?"

One of the villagers, in a sort of archaic Bengali, replied, "This is the village of Sharfarali."

"What other villages are around? How do you make a living?"

"Babu, the villages of Jangalkhas, Salman and Abruagunj lie adjacent to our village. Surely, you must have heard about our cotton textiles. They are famous and exported across the world from the Sonargaon port, along with our molasses and handmade *madurkathi* mats. We also grow rice, jute and sugar cane."

Isa was impressed.

"Do the Mogs or the Harmads attack these areas?"

"Can anyone in Bengal be safe from them? That is why we stay in the jungles in small enclosures. But the firangis come from Sylhet and they need to cross the zamindar's palace first, where the sentries are always on alert."

Isa got interested.

"Which mahal are we talking of? Where does it stand?"

The villager looked at Isa with disdain.

"Have you not heard of Jongol Badi, the palace of the Koch rulers? It lies around ten koshes north-east from here."

So, Isa and his men proceeded towards Jongol Badi. As they made their way through the jungle, it suddenly cleared and they gaped at a palace, probably spread over fifty bighas, with a three hundred feet moat surrounding it. There was a drawbridge on the southern side and as Isa approached the palace, he wondered whether he was entering an abandoned mansion. For no one was to be seen.

The news of Isa's announcement at Chandpratap that he would punish anyone who betrayed Bengal had been communicated far and near. Therefore, as Isa approached Jongol Badi, their rulers—Ram Hazra and Lakshman Hazra—who were paying their taxes to the Mughals, thought that Isa had come to punish them. They decided it was better to flee rather than face Isa and hastily retreated through the subterranean tunnel, which lay beneath the eastern part of the ditch.

Isa was pleasantly surprised to walk into an empty palace. *What a good place to rule from, surrounded by thick forests with numerous distributaries of the Brahmaputra flowing across. All I need is a good fort at the opening of the river to keep vigil on the enemies. I will rule from Jongol Badi, while Musa would reign from Sarail and Karimullah could govern from Sonargaon. That way, the Sripur Roys would have no incentive to attack Sonargaon.* Isa chuckled to himself as the thoughts ran through his mind. He muttered, "I hope Karimullah has been able to reconquer Sonargaon."

Karimullah, in the meantime, had approached Sonargaon. There was no movement anywhere and he felt the Mughals must have abandoned the town. As he directed his kosha closer to the port city for his men to disembark, he spotted the cannons trained at the kosha. He immediately ordered his men to move full blast ahead because that was the only way of saving the kosha.

As the first shots were fired, the kosha picked up speed and the fire balls flew over them. The kosha was now going at well-nigh full speed, and Karimullah knew that by the time the Mughals repositioned the cannons, they would have taken the bend in the river. But what bothered him was that if the Katrabo Fort had fallen, it was equally likely that the Idrakpuri Fort too had fallen. If cannons were fired from Idrakpuri Fort too, and they again accelerated to avoid the shots, they would enter the Padma where the kosha would be a sitting duck for the guns of Sripur.

So, Karimullah decided it was best to stop and recce the surrounding before proceeding further. A deafening crackling noise filled the air as the kosha was grounded. Karimullah was sure the keel had snapped. The men were rattled but safe.

Karimullah and his men banked on the opposite side of Sonargaon. He quickly shouted out an instruction, "Stay away from the riverbank!"

As they proceeded to camp, they found their soldiers from the Katrabo Fort approaching them, attracted by the loud noise. Karimullah was happy to see them, for he had feared that they were lost.

One of the soldiers declared, "Senapati, Katrabo Fort has fallen and Rakhal was killed defending it."

Karimullah was pained to hear the death of Rakhal and three other sentries. He prayed his death was not a signal of looming darkness.

"What about the Idrakpuri Fort?" Karimullah asked with great trepidation.

"We have that, Senapati."

The plan was set in action. Today, there would be a great party near the riverfront. All the soldiers would make merry, so that their singing and dancing could be heard from the fort. In the meanwhile, Karimullah and two dozen soldiers would cross the river and attack the fort through the secret underground tunnel. Once the fort was captured, they would place a torch on the eastern side, and that would be the signal for the rest of the soldiers to abandon their partying and cross the river.

As expected, the Mughal sentries were distracted by the celebration in the enemy camp. Karimullah and his men quietly entered the basement of the fort, quickly moved up the stairs, swiftly overpowered the guards and instantly killed them.

A dozen men stayed back at the tower, positioning the cannons on the enemy barracks, while Karimullah and the rest of his men moved downstairs to eliminate the rest of the soldiers. Most of the Mughal soldiers were fast asleep and bled to death even before they understood that they had been attacked, and when Karimullah saw that the rest of his soldiers had crossed the river, he ordered the cannons to be fired. The Mughal soldiers in the barracks ran helter-skelter, and most of them were chased and killed by Isa's men. By morning, Sonargaon was recaptured and Karimullah himself set out to inform Isa of the victory.

It was late afternoon when he reached Karimpur Ghat. He saw the army of Masum Khan Kabuli camping there and was informed that the Mughal army had camped there yesterday.

"Isa Khan is now occupying Jongol Badi," Masum informed him. Karimullah immediately realised that the opportune time to attack Shahbaz had come.

He requested Masum, "Be ready for the battle on the outskirts of Jongol Badi with muskets. Please saddle a few muskets on my horse."

As he journeyed through the night, he saw the Mughal forces camping outside the forest, but he made his way through the thick jungle, hoping he was not attacked by any wild beast, and he reached the palace early in the morning.

Isa was thrilled to see Karimullah and warmly embraced him. "You have not slept for two nights. You need rest. Go and sleep for my sake!"

"I have spent nights without sleeping when I was the shah's bodyguard. More important deeds await us now. Sleep can wait."

Thus, Isa and Karimullah, along with their soldiers, proceeded to meet Shahbaz and his men. They spread wide and moved silently, like when a hunter approaches his prey, and when they heard footsteps, they immediately halted to take their position. Each one picked their target, and at Karimullah's hand wave, twenty bullets flew and at least a dozen Mughals fell. It was difficult to gallop or charge on horses in a forest, so Shahbaz panicked and told his men to withdraw, but Isa had his men continue to fire at them. A few more of his men fell, but the time intervals between loading the muskets and firing gave the Mughals a window to escape.

But as they came out in the open, guns fired from the southern side. Masum Khan's men had also taken up position. Hundreds of Mughals fell, and Shahbaz now decided it was best to retreat. But he and his men were now pursued by Isa's army.

Isa managed to send a message to Masum to go and capture the Mughal cannons that were on their way to Karimpur Ghat.

Shahbaz Khan fled, but he still could not understand how his best military plan had failed. He had attacked Isa in stealth, quickly captured Sonargaon, but in less than a week, the tables had been turned. His friend Chand Ghazi was dead, and when he thought he had Isa cornered, he came with muskets to outsmart him, and now, Isa presided over both Jongol Badi and Sonargaon. Shahbaz wondered what he would tell Emperor Akbar. Everyone complained about him as he was a staunch arrogant Sunni, but Akbar tolerated him because he was a good general. Yet he had failed to capture Maharana Pratap and now he had been disgraced by Isa Khan.

As Shahbaz prepared for his long journey to Fatehpur Sikri, the Bhati region erupted in joy. Isa requested all the leading zamindars of Bhati to assemble at Jongol Badi a week after Jamai Shashthi to celebrate the momentous occasion.

22

The Suicide

How could Kedar accept Isa's invitation?

As the thought ran through Chand's mind, he cursed the day Sona was born. He cursed the day he introduced Ramdas to Sridhara. He cursed Isa Khan. *This is how my daughter is thanking me for loving her?*

Deboki entered the room and saw her distraught husband.

"You have turned pale and look sick. What has happened to you?"

Chand was almost in tears.

"I do not know what to do! Isa is going from strength to strength and each of his victory is another slap on my face. I was the upholder of Bengali Kulinism for the last three decades and now my beloved daughter is happily married to Isa. How can I now show my face in the Kulin Kayastha community?"

"Calm down. There's nothing we can do now ..."

"I have always prided that there are only another three-and-a-half Kulin Kayasthas in south-east Bengal—the Basus of Malkhanagar, the Guhas/Mustafis of Srinagar, the Ghoshes of Pailodia and the half-Kulin Duttas of Kathalia. Yet, I have not been able to protect my own house. We tried to attack Sonargaon, but Isa has always proved too strong for us. And now, with the defeat of Shahbaz Khan, Isa has virtually become the de facto ruler of Bengal!"

Chand paused to collect himself.

"And now the unthinkable has happened. He has invited all the leading zamindars to celebrate his victory, and Kedar has agreed to visit! Can you believe that? My own brother! Does Kedar not understand the repercussions? People will taunt me! This means I have accepted a Mussalman as my *damad*."

"What can Kedar do? If he has to live in Bengal, he has to sign the truce with Isa. See what Isa did to Chand Ghazi and his family whom he thought were collaborating with the Mughals. I can tell you, Kedar must have reached this decision after a lot of deliberation. Kedar has forgiven Isa for the time being, but he has not forgotten the humiliation. I am sure, this truce with Isa is just a facade and he will retaliate at the right time."

"I hope you are right. But you know, Deboki, what intrigues me most is the cruel twists of fate. I facilitated the meeting of Ramdas and Sridhara, due to which Isa was traced and rescued. In that meeting held on the day of Sona's annaprashan, I pitied Sridhara since he had ordered the extermination of his son, Pratapaditya. Yet today, Pratapaditya is well and alive. On the other hand, my beloved daughter has become a blot in my life! I could so do with some wise counsel now."

"Why don't you consult Raja Jagadananda Roy of Chandradwip?"

"You are right. I will send a messenger to Chandradwip and take the advice of my dear friend Jagadananda."

Chand called for his trusted physician Raghunandan Das and said, "Normally, I would have sent Sanatan to Chandradwip but I do not trust him any more. I feel he had a role to play in Sona's abduction. Yet, I have no *sabut*. I can retire him, but he knows too much of our estate and our operations. I am afraid that if I banish him, he can go and trade our secrets with the Mughals or Isa and expose us. I therefore continue to retain his services while watching him closely. Therefore, in this time of our misfortune, it is only you I can look forward to as my trusted lieutenant. Please carry this letter to Jagadananda and seek his advice!"

Raghunandan left immediately and returned in two days. It was early morning when he arrived in Sripur.

He ran into Chand who was on his way to the temple.

"You have returned rather quickly Raghunandan. What advice do you bring from Jagadananda?"

Raghunandan sighed.

"Sir, Jagadananda is no more!"

"What do you mean?"

"Bhowmik *moshai*, it was almost midnight when I approached Chandradwip, but the boatsmen refused to go further, saying it was unnatural for the water to be so quiet on a summer night. I tried to persuade them, but they were adamant. Shortly afterwards, I could understand why!"

"I saw gigantic waves approaching, the kind I have never seen in my life. The waves were taller than fifty elephants. It appeared that a huge sea mammoth had awakened and was rushing towards us, engulfing anything in its path. I thank the *prabhu* that I was in a big boat, for any other boat would have capsized. We survived because of the skills of the coxswain, who steered the boat to mid-water before changing directions from starboard to meet the waves head on."

Raghunandan paused for a while, shaking his head as if to erase the dreadful memory. "Boat rides have never made me nauseous. But for once, I was. I clung to the mast to steady myself but soon started vomiting. Even a few of the seasoned crew were vomiting. I just kept on chanting Lord Shiva's name for what seemed an eternity, but which I am told was for only thirty minutes. And then normalcy returned.

"We took a while to clean ourselves and the boat. As we finally progressed towards Chandrawip, we could see debris and destruction all around. It appeared that the entire island had been devastated. We anchored close to the shore and waited for dawn. On alighting at the island in the morning, I saw corpses lying all around.

"Suddenly, Raja Kandarpanarayan Roy approached us. I told him I had come as your emissary, but he was distraught. He told me that he had been able to survive by clinging on to a tree, but they could not find his father. An hour later, they recovered Jagadananda's body from the Ganga. It appears the waves had plucked Jagadananda from his bed and plunged him into the Ganga! Sir, I am sorry for bringing you such bad news."

"Raghunandan, why should you be sorry? You were just doing your duty. I am grateful to you for bringing such news to me at the earliest. Now, let me go and pray."

As Chand prayed hard, he reflected, *Maybe I never really loved Sona as she was. Did I ever try to understand her? Living the life of a vidhawa must have been terrible for someone of her age. The cross was too heavy for her to bear. I need to stop looking at the world from my viewpoint.*

He took out his white shawl. He looked all around but there was no one. He climbed a tree, strung the shawl as a noose around his neck and hanged himself.

A few minutes later, the shrill shriek of a maid woke up the entire Raj Badi. Kedar rushed out of his room and saw a maid screaming in fright near Keshaber Mar Dighi. He hastily made his way there, only to see the hanging corpse of his brother. He immediately climbed up to loosen the noose, but his brother was dead. The mighty Chand Roy was no more.

As Kedar lit the funeral pyre, he muttered, "Dada, you were like my baba. I am what I am today because of you. I understand your angst. I hope you will forgive me!"

As the fire kindled and engulfed the corpse, and chants of "Hare Ram" filled the air, Kedar suppressed his tears and screamed, "Dada!"

23

The Grand Feast

IT WAS THE DAY OF Jamai Shashti. Sona stepped into Jongol Badi for the first time. Karimullah had gone to escort her to Isa's new capital. As she crossed the moat, she saw Isa standing to welcome her.

"Finally, I have reached. I almost thought that you had instructed Karimullah to take me inside the deep jungles and finish me off!"

Isa looked at Sona with disbelief.

"Sona, how can you talk like that? Do you not know that I love you more than anything else and am prepared to fight the whole world for your sake?"

Sona smiled.

"Jaan, I was only teasing you. How can I even have any negative thoughts about you that too on Jamai Shashthi when sons-in-law are pampered? You gave me a second life and showed me how to live it."

"You must be tired after such a long arduous journey. Let me show you to the inner chambers and you can get a well-deserved rest."

As they proceeded, Sona winked at Isa, and asked, "Do you really want me to rest?"

Isa's face reddened with embarrassment. Sona loved whenever Isa's face turned crimson red because it made him look so vulnerable. "Sona, you are expecting. Such a long journey is not recommended during pregnancy, and you need all the rest."

As they settled in the inner quarters, Isa asked, "So how long have you been pregnant?"

"Maybe three months. But you keep such a check on my cycles, you are so always on top of everything, that I thought you would be the one coming and informing me that I needed to go and check with a hakim."

"Sona, I have been preoccupied with the raids and was wondering how to stop the attacks from Sripur, and probably therefore failed to notice."

Then his eyes gleamed.

"At least, for the next few months, I cannot be on top of everything."

Sona was embarrassed and blushed.

Isa guffawed, put his lips on Sona's belly and whispered, "My child, are you a boy or a girl?"

"I am sure it will be a boy. He will have your handsome looks and your strength, and will be successful—just like you—in war and love."

"But I already have a son, and I would love to have a daughter as beautiful as you, who would give us solace in our dotage!"

Sona's eyes saddened.

"I have been a disgrace to my parents. I have only caused grief to them. I do not want another Sona!"

"You did nothing wrong. You gave love a chance. While your parents may have abandoned you, you continue to think of their well-being. But why feel sad when we are excited about a bright future? So, tell me, why do you think that our child will be a son?"

"I have heard from midwives that if you have conceived a girl, you will have morning sickness in the first three months. But except for one episode of morning sickness, I have not experienced any uneasiness and hence I am convinced it is a boy."

"Surely, that cannot be a way to determine the gender of a child!"

Isa paused and enquired, "Would you mind if I call Fatima over to Jongol Badi? I feel her experience can be a great support to you during the next few months."

"Most certainly!"

But, with a twinkle in her eye, she asked, "Are you calling her over so that you can spend time with her, knowing that I will be complaining as I go into the final months of pregnancy?"

Isa grabbed Sona's wrist and replied, "You distrustful lady, you need to be taught a lesson!"

Isa instantly pinned Sona's hands behind her, gently lay her down on the bed and urgently started kissing her. Sona responded vigorously. Their tongues interlocked, he started fondling her breasts, while she rubbed her hands over his chest and abdomen. She felt Isa stiffening and moved her hands down to feel his throbbing manhood. She grabbed his manhood with both hands and started caressing it, and she could sense Isa was ready to plunge into her. She was also wet, but they were lying sideways and she realised it would be difficult for Isa to penetrate her. Seeing that Isa was not taking the initiative on getting on top of her, she mounted Isa and guided him into her.

As Sona bounced on Isa, she realised that being on top had a different pleasure. She could control the movements and pace her climax as she desired. Isa watched with fascination as Sona rocked up and down, first slowly and then vigorously. She seemed to be transported into a world of frenzied excitement until she came.

As Isa felt Sona go down on him, he smiled contentedly and reflected, *Sona's pregnancy will most certainly not compromise on our lovemaking*!

Isa started preparation for the big feast he was planning the next weekend for the bhuiyans of Bengal. He ensured Brahmin cooks were brought in, as also halal meat, so that neither Muslims nor Hindus could complain their religion was compromised. He also encouraged his Portuguese soldiers, especially Carvalho and Gonsalves, to source the choicest vegetables that were unknown to Bengal. He wanted the celebration to be a bigger success than what he had experienced in Sripur. He debated whether to send invitation to the Tipperah kingdom, wondering whether the rani would feel slighted if he did not invite her in person, and then decided he would visit them once his child was born to make her the child's guardian mother.

Fatima arrived before the guests. Isa quickly took her to Sona's room, and the two warmly hugged each other.

"Didi, I am so relieved that you are here. My morning sickness has increased and I feel miserable. I feel like crying all the time. Isa is always so busy with all important matters that I have no one to share my thoughts with. I miss Achala like anything, but she had to go back to Sonargaon as her family stays there."

"Even I had a terrible time when Musa was born. I did not realise I was expecting for the first four months and felt pregnancy was a breeze. But the next five months was tortuous. I believe, if you have conceived a girl, the first few months are painful, while a son will cause agony in the last few months before birth, just like they cause misery in your later life!"

Sona glared at Fatima.

"Didi, what are you saying? It is girls who make their parents suffer!"

Fatima was quick to counter.

"You should have seen the despondency in my *saas* when her sons were captured. Their absence kept her dispirited. Further, when Isa returned, he hardly spent time with her which made her even more disheartened. It seemed, his mind was somewhere else. His irritability made him shout at my saas on a few occasions. Let me tell you, Sona bibi, that sons are ungrateful!"

Sona reflected on Fatima's statement. She looked forward to meeting her uncle Kedar when he arrived later in the day, for she was appraised that he, along with the leading zamindars of Bengal, were arriving in the afternoon.

Pratapaditya and Masum Khan were the first to arrive. Isa welcomed them and escorted them to the *mehmaan khana*. Shortly afterwards, Isa was surprised to find Kedar Roy with a clean-shaven head approaching him and rushed to him. He asked, "Why have you shaved your head?"

"Isa, my brother committed suicide because he could not bear the ignominy of his daughter being abducted by a Mussalman."

"I am so sorry to hear this. May his soul be in peace. Kedar, I love your niece and I can promise you her happiness is the most important thing to me."

"I am supporting you for the cause of Bengal. But I have no love lost towards you."

As all the guests assembled and feasted on the delicacies, Isa announced, "I invited all of you here to tell you that I am deeply committed to the spirit of an undivided Bhati. The Mughals can rule till Tanda, but here, our voice is supreme. We will fight the invaders, whether they are Mughals, Mogs or Harmads, tooth and nail, and to do that, I require all of your support!"

The guests burst into loud cheers and claps.

Suddenly, Isa saw Sona beckoning to him from the inside. He rushed indoors.

"Why has my uncle shaved his hair? Has anyone died in our family?"

"Sona, your father is no more."

Sona let out a scream in pain.

"How did my father die?"

Isa hugged her to calm her down.

"He took his own life."

As wails erupted from Sona, Fatima barged into the room.

"Congratulations Isa! I have been trying to catch you since the time I saw Sona getting up from her afternoon siesta. She stepped out of the room with her right foot. You will have a son!"

24

The Road Ahead

THIS ISA IS A REAL pain in the neck. Unless I quickly bring him under control, the collective strength of these Bengali chieftains will expand rapidly. I thought Maharana Pratap of Mewar was my biggest thorn, but now it looks Isa Khan is my biggest worry.

As the thoughts raged through Emperor Akbar's mind, he hardly realised that he had barged into his favourite wife Mariam's room.

It was the autumn of 1584. The scorching heat of the summer was behind, as was the sticky humidity of the monsoon. Within a few days, the neighbourhood would erupt to the vibrant festivities of Diwali, lighting up in a burst of colours and sounds. While the crème de la crème looked forward to the royal banquet, the commoners awaited the generosity of the emperor. Everyone eagerly looked forward to the upcoming celebrations except the person whose religious tolerance had made Diwali such a popular festival in the capital city of Agra. Abu'l-Fath Jalal-ud-Din Muhammad Akbar had reasons to be a worried man.

It was almost three decades since Akbar had ascended the throne at the tender age of thirteen. He had understood early in life that territorial expansion would not only increase the security of his kingdom, but also boost the economic power of his kingdom by providing access to more resources, such as fertile land, minerals, trade routes and strategic locations. Akbar could look back with pride on how he had consolidated his power in India by subjugating his formidable adversaries—the fiercely independent Rajputs were formidable adversaries—through both military and diplomatic approaches.

Akbar recollected the discussions he had with his commander Bairam Khan as they marched towards Delhi after the Second Battle of Panipat way back in 1556. This had followed barely after a year of the Battle of Sirhind in which Emperor Humayun's troops had destroyed Sikandar Shah Suri's army.

"Khan-i-Khanan, how come the enemy was able to regroup so quickly, albeit under their Hindu commander Hemu, and capture Delhi the moment Abbu died?"

Bairam's words still resonated with Akbar.

"Mian, the capital of Delhi is financed by the granary of the east. By the time your father understood the same, Sher Shah had seized suzerainty of Bengal. With the funds available at his disposal, Sher Shah could buy as many mercenary soldiers as needed. Meanwhile, your father's finances dwindled and he was not able to pay his soldiers on time, which left his army disgruntled. Hence, his position weakened. You need to have control of Bengal for your revenues. Which will help you in funding your military missions. Just imagine the kind of wealth Bengal gives access to which enabled the Suris to regroup so quickly. The ride to Delhi starts from Bengal!"

Akbar reflected, *Bengal needs to be totally controlled at the earliest ...*

"What's troubling you, my beloved Jalal-ud-Din?"

Mariam-uz-Zamani was surprised at the unexpected visit as the emperor usually presided over his court during this time. Born Harkha Bai to Raja Bharmal of Amber, Mariam had married Akbar when both were twenty years old, and over the years she had come to know the shahenshah so well that she could now read him like the back of her hand. She was also the mother of Akbar's eldest son and the heir apparent, Prince Salim.

Mariam looked up at the emperor, as he approached her divan, dragging his leg left slightly. Excessive horse riding in his childhood had left his limbs somewhat bowed inwards. Mariam loved gazing at his eyes but today, the spark was missing from them. Mariam could make out Akbar was disconcerted.

What worried Akbar was uprisings in Bengal. Conquering the Rajputana territories in the western part of his empire had a heavy toll on his exchequer. Ordinarily, these would have been financed by revenue collections from Bengal, but there was disquiet in the far eastern territory of his regime. The revenue slowdown in Bengal for the Mughals was aiding the local landlords there and making them stronger.

Akbar knew he had to send troops immediately so that the rebels could be vanquished before the monsoon sets in, else his army could face the same fate as his last governor Shahbaz Khan's army.

"Shahbaz Khan has failed in his mission to capture Bengal and has now returned to Fatehpur Sikri. Over the last few years, I have sent so many governors to Bengal—Khan Jahan, Muzaffar Khan Turbati, Mirza Aziz and now Shahbaz Khan—but all of them have failed to reign in the rebels. All these subahdars complained of a group of twelve Bengali zamindars called Baro Bhuiyans who had become too powerful and rebellious, but their chief grouse is against Isa Khan. I am at a loss what to do now!"

The beautiful Mariam wickedly grinned.

"Aren't you thankful to the Rajputs for providing you so many beautiful ladies like me? Why, even two of your Navratnas are Rajputs—Raja Man Singh and Raja Todar Mal."

"Mariam, you know you are my favourite. Yes, I was barely twenty years old when I was campaigning all the time in Rajputana. Thankfully, I learnt early on during my first campaign against Rana Pratap of Mewar that controlling Rajputana through outright subjugation could be difficult. Hence, I have subsequently followed a policy of integration through diplomacy, alliances and strategic marriages. But, what is your point, Mariam?"

"What is there to think about? Send your precious Navaratna to Bengal with a large battalion. My *bhatija* has successfully governed Kabul and decimated Afghan rebels there in the past, now let him go eastward and destroy the local resistance there."

"You are so right, Begum! I will immediately ask Man Singh to proceed towards Bengal. Isa Khan, your end is near!"

Thus, Man Singh, son of Raja Bhagwant Das and nephew of Mariam-uz-Zamani, was appointed the new subahdar of Bengal. He set out for Tanda with over ten thousand men and over one hundred cannons. His instruction was clear—"Defeat Isa Khan and bring Bengal under Mughal dominion."

Man Singh reached Tanda just as the monsoon ended. He immediately called a meeting with the platoon commanders who had accompanied Shahbaz Khan in his earlier missions and asked them, "Why do you think you failed in your earlier missions?"

Ali, a platoon commander, responded, "Subahdar, we thought we would win on both the occasions we confronted the bhuiyans; whenever we attacked, they turned and fled—and like cats chasing mice, we followed them. But just when we thought we had them cornered and victory was near, they turned back, and we realised we had fallen into their trap! Last time, they even seized our artillery as we ran helter-skelter."

Man Singh was fascinated by the accounts he heard, and realised this had to be a well-planned campaign. Studying the maps, he enquired, "Who are the key rebels?"

"The key person is Isa Khan. He rules over Sarail, Sonargaon and the Koch region, but it is very difficult to predict his whereabouts. He knows the region and its rivers exceedingly well. You attack him in Sarail, and you will find he has escaped to Sonargaon. You attack him in Sonargaon, he will retreat by the river; you chase him on the river, suddenly he will disappear through a distributary; and when you are wondering where he has vanished, he will attack you from behind!"

Man Singh listened to Ali with rapt attention.

"Can you show me on the *naqshah* where these places are?"

As Ali identified the locations, Man Singh marked the spots with an ink pen. "Who are the other revolting zamindars?"

"Masum Khan of Pabna would be another key adversary, along with Pratapaditya of Barisal. Raja Lakshman Manikya of Bhuluya and Kandarpanarayan of Chandradwip do not pay taxes but they are on the extreme borders of the Bhati region. If we conquer Bhati, they will start paying taxes. The other three who could be dangerous are Raja Kangsanarayan Laskar Roy of Taharpur, Fazl Ghazi of Bhawal and Kedar Roy of Sripur. We still do not know where their loyalties lie."

"I gathered that Isa Khan abducted the daughter of Chand Roy, due to which he committed suicide. Will the Sripur Roy support Isa?"

"True, Isa Khan abducted and married Chand Roy's daughter, and she is expecting. I would have said the Sripur Roys would not support Isa if Chand was alive, but I gather Kedar Roy attended the assembly that Isa organised in summer."

"Send your spies and find out where Chand Roy's daughter is residing. That is where we will attack because I am sure Isa will be in her vicinity. But before we plan our approach, can you point out the locations of these other bhuiyans, and indicate the various fortifications that Isa has?"

"Isa has forts in Katrabo, Kalaigachha, Khizirpur, Idrakpuri, Murapara, Dewanbagh, Egarasindur, Sherpur, Dasa Kahania and Rangamati."

As Ali started pointing out these forts, Man Singh realised he was facing a formidable foe and he needed to draw the enemy out to attack him, which meant it would be a long-drawn siege of attrition.

He called his men.

"Tomorrow, we leave for Bhati. We will build our defences here near Gazipur. We will use this place as our base to attack Isa and we must be prepared for a long haul. Hence, it is imperative to ensure two prerequisites—a strong navy which can challenge Isa during the monsoon season, and fresh supply of water and food to sustain us during this long campaign. Procuring food will not be a problem, but we need to dig a large *talab* which will ensure undisrupted water supply to our men."

Thus, Man Singh and his ten-thousand-strong army proceeded to Bhati and pitched their tent in Demra where his men dug a large tank and named it Gangasagar. The surroundings were cleared of all projections and named Rajarbagh.

Meanwhile, Isa was tense as he strolled in the corridors of Jongol Badi, wondering when he could leave to inspect Man Singh's forces. Sona was in labour and the midwife had come, but Sona seemed to be in terrible distress. Almost an hour had passed, when the door to Sona's room opened. Isa rushed to the door and asked, "Any news?"

The midwife shrugged.

"Niyamat bibi is troubled. She has to relax otherwise there could be complications!"

Isa rushed into the room.

"Sona, are you fine? What ails you?"

"Whenever I close my eyes to go into labour, the face of my father appears. He scorns me for marrying a Muslim and disgracing our family honour, cursing me that any progeny of ours will rot in *jahannum*. On seeing his face and hearing his admonitions, all contractions cease!"

"People who have settled outside their provinces tend to cling on to their religion and heritage more assiduously. When I was in Qazvin, every Muslim was an equal and no one compared whether one was Ashraf or Ajlaf. Here, Man Singh—a staunch Hindu Rajput is attacking us on behalf of Akbar, but his paternal aunt, Akbar's favourite begum, is a Muslim. No one condemns interfaith marriages there, but here in Bengal, everyone wears religion on their sleeves.

"I am indeed sorry that your father took his life unable to bear the disgrace, but that was the influence of the parochial society we belong to. I want Bengal to transcend from these religious sentiments and unite for the betterment of the society.

"We are expecting our first child, a product of our love. Akbar and Mariam's child is a product of their love from a mixed marriage, and he is destined to be the next emperor. Our first child should also receive all our blessings and support and I pray he is the guiding star who unites all religions in Bengal."

Sona held on to Isa's hands and murmured, "You are a *chhupa rustam*! You always know how to prevail over me."

Sona tightened her grasp on Isa and then let out a loud scream. Seconds later, the midwife announced, "Congratulations Isa saheb! You have been blessed with a son."

Isa kissed the forehead of his baby and remarked, "Let him be named Adom, our first, for he will be the forerunner of this region."

Then, kissing Sona, he said, "Jaan, I need to depart for the battlefield as the Mughals are advancing on us."

Isa set for Dewanbagh as it was the closest fort to the vicinity of Rajarbagh. From there, he took a small retinue of soldiers to go and inspect the Mughal forces closer. Looking at their encampment, Isa reflected, *It would be unwise to go in for a guerrilla warfare. I have to take the enemy head-on.*

He sent for an emissary and said, "Send your men to Sonargaon, Sarail, Bhawal, Sripur, Jessore, Chandradwip, Bhuluya, Bhushana and other areas, and ask their men to join us at Egarasindur. This will be the final battle. Meanwhile, let me attempt a diversion so that we buy time to meet them."

Isa chose Egarasindur for two reasons. It was at the corner of the Bhati region, just bordering his palace on the Meghna River. This would probably be the farthest the Mughals needed to travel from Demra to meet him at one of his strongholds. If Egarasindur fell, they could quickly retreat through the jungles into Jongol Badi, and escape from its underground tunnel into the wilderness of Sylhet. Thus, Egarasindur was the only place that provided him a safe retreat while facing the Mughal army in full strength.

Isa realised he had to delay Man Singh's movement to Jongol Badi, or else he could not confront him there. He let it be known that he was camping at Dewanbagh, and he was pleased to see the next day Man Singh's army encircling Dewanbagh. The cannons of Man Singh's army roared, Isa's men fired a few shots, and then they escaped the fort through the underground tunnel. As Isa looked back, he saw the Mughals making a triumphant entry into the Dewanbagh Fort.

The final battle was now awaiting at Egarasindur. Isa had got the necessary respite, and his armies from Sarail and Sonargaon were now with him. As Man Singh's men approached the Meghna, Isa scanned the Mughal army in the company of Karimullah and Musa. He lamented, "The enmity of the Mughal is with me. If we fight this battle, a lot of innocent lives will be lost."

The next day, as both armies prepared for war, an envoy reached Man Singh, carrying a letter from Isa.

"Subahdar Man Singh—I realise you and your emperor's enmity is against me. Why should the poor soldiers suffer because of our animosity? Let the two of us only battle, and may the winner be victorious!"

Man Singh acquiesced.

The two skilled warriors fought for hours, befitting their skills, which enamoured the soldiers. Then, Man Singh's sword broke. Isa stopped in his tracks. He thought, *Man Singh, for all his valour and skills, deserves another chance.*

But Man Singh refused to pick up another sword.

Why does Man Singh want to enter into a manual combat with me? Isa too discarded his sword and waited for Man

Singh to approach him. Instead, Man Singh genuflected and offered his right hand.

"From childhood, I have heard the story of Alexander and Porus, how Alexander the conqueror tried to vanquish Porus, and how Porus stubbornly defended himself. To us Rajputs, Porus is our hero. You remind me of Porus, and for long, people in Bhati will respect and sing about your valour and glory!

"As Akbar's representative here, I can only assure you this. Become our ally, continue to protect Bengal as an independent ruler while aligning with us, and we will support you from enemy threats. You are a king and deserve to be treated like one!"

Isa looked up towards Jongol Badi. Sona had just been blessed with a son, the future looked bright and as he stood there, he recollected Pari's prophecy, "The slave one day will become a king!"

He stepped forward and clasped Man Singh's outstretched hand.

Acknowledgements

I ALWAYS WANTED TO WRITE a book on the Baro Bhuiyans and in 2016, I mentioned this to my batchmate and then neighbour Rohan Singhal. Over the next four years, Rohan would routinely follow up on the progress of my book, and I would try to evade the topic. However, when the pandemic started, I promptly enrolled in David Wheeler's course "Write Your First Novel". Over the next twenty-six weeks, I was successful in completing the first draft of my debut novel. Thank you, David, and my batchmates there for their constant encouragement. Rohan, I owe this book to you.

I am forever grateful to my family, friends and well-wishers, for their unwavering support throughout this journey.

First and foremost, I owe a special debt of gratitude to my parents, Ivy and Sankar Nath Som, whose immense love and unshakable belief in me have shaped who I am today. My father's inputs on the manuscript have been invaluable.

To my ever-encouraging, understanding and patient wife Shilpi Datta Som for being my biggest supporter. I could not have completed this book without your constant encouragement.

And my children, Aditya and Ishani, you are my pillars of strength. Your boundless energy, laughter and curiosity remind me daily of the importance of storytelling and imagination. I hope this book inspires you to chase your dreams.

Pradipta Prasun Saha and Narayan Iyer, your critical feedback on the initial chapters has greatly helped the book.

Thank you Nandini Vijayraghavan for bringing Suhail Mathur of The Book Bakers into my life. Without Suhail and his talented team, my long-cherished dream would not have turned into reality.

I am immensely grateful to Ajay Mago, publisher, Om Books International, and Chief Editor Shantanu Ray Chaudhuri for believing in the book.

A special thank you to Jyotsna Mehta whose expertise and insights helped shape this book into what it is today. It was a great privilege and an honour to have you as my editor.

Finally, to all the readers. I hope this book resonates with you as much as it has with me.